WHAT MOTHER WON'T TELL ME

IVAR LEON MENGER

Translated by Jamie Bulloch
Adaptation editor Thomas Scholz

For my daughter, Ava

Cover design and illustration by Spencer Fuller/Faceout Studio
Background texture by siloto/Shutterstock
Internal design by Laura Boren/Sourcebooks

Originally published as *Als das Böse kam*, © Ivar Leon Menger, 2022. Translated from German by Jamie Bulloch.

Published by Poisoned Pen Press, an imprint of Sourcebooks
P.O. Box 4410, Naperville, Illinois 60567-4410
(630) 961-3900
sourcebooks.com

Originally published as *Als das Böse kam* in 2022 in Germany by dtv Verlagsgesellschaft.

Cataloging-in-Publication Data is on file with the Library of Congress.

Printed and bound in the United States of America.
LSC 10 9 8 7 6 5 4 3 2 1

PRAISE FOR *WHAT MOTHER WON'T TELL ME*

"*What Mother Won't Tell Me* starts off as the eerie, captivating story of a girl raised in isolation from the outside world—then takes a hairpin turn into full-blown horror-thriller territory. Menger's story brings all the menace of classic fairy tales into the modern world. The tension ratchets up and never lets go. This is an intoxicating novel, well worth the sleep you will lose as you read 'just one more chapter.'"

—Clémence Michallon, international bestselling author of *The Quiet Tenant*

"Tension leaps off the pages in this page-turning domestic thriller."

—Mary Burton, *New York Times* bestselling author

"This heart-pounding thriller draws on elements of Hansel and Gretel, *Mommie Dearest*, and ripped-from-the-headlines crime to render a wholly unique, gripping tale. The sympathetic narrator, beautiful prose, and page-turning pace is sure to make readers forget whatever else they're doing so they can keep reading. A heart-stopping, surprising, lyrical, and thrilling read."

—Sharon Short, author of *Trouble Island*

"*What Mother Won't Tell Me* is a perfect thriller—wholly original, haunting, riveting, and relentlessly suspenseful. Start reading this one early, or I guarantee you'll be up all night."

—Jason Starr, author of *The Next Time I Die*

She began to cry bitterly…
for she could see nothing but water…
and no way of reaching the land.

HANS CHRISTIAN ANDERSEN

PART ONE

1

Mother is in the kitchen baking a blueberry cake. The house smells of warm caramel, even though all the doors and windows are wide open. Outside, a blue bird chirps slowly. A summer wind breezes through the rooms, bringing a pleasant relief from the afternoon heat spreading through our prison.

I've put on an apron, and I help Mother wash up while Boy sets the table for coffee in the dining room. "What are we going to play today?" I ask, putting the clean mixing bowl back in the cupboard.

"Monopoly?" Mother replies, shooting me a mischievous glance. We know how Father has a fit if he lands on one of our hotels. The board goes flying, and it rains banknotes. Boy and I love it when that happens.

But we'll have to play something else today.

To make sure my plan works.

"Shall I get out Risk?" I say as casually as possible. Mother frowns. She hates that game. There's a reason she hides the cardboard box at the bottom of her chest of drawers in their bedroom. Probably in the hopes that my brother and I will forget we've got it.

"That's a very silly game," Mother says, putting down the drying-up cloth and crossing her arms. "Haven't we told you that violence never solves conflict?" She looks at me seriously. "Peace and freedom are precious, Juno. Our family lives with enough fear as it is here."

"But it's such fun," I lie, thrusting my hands in the sewed-on front pocket of my Sunday dress. My right forefinger is already wiggling like a worm in a bird's beak. It's done that since I was a little girl. Whenever I don't tell the truth. I can't control it.

"It also teaches us to think strategically. You have to make the right decisions when you're attacked." I'm getting into my stride. "In case the strangers appear on our island. Father's keen that we can defend ourselves."

"What am I keen on?" Father says, carrying a bundle of firewood into the kitchen. He puts on gloves, opens the firebox to the wood stove and adds another log. "That smells absolutely delicious."

"Your daughter wants to play Risk," Mother says.

"Great idea!" Boy says, rushing into the room, flinging open the cutlery drawer and taking out the cake server and four forks.

"I'm up for that," Father says, putting my brother in a headlock. "But watch out, my son, I'm going to get you!" They tussle and tickle each other mercilessly.

I watch Mother untie her apron, lay it over the back of a chair and smooth the creases with her hand. I get the sense she's not thrilled by my suggestion. She probably expected a different reaction from Father. She shakes her head. Maybe she's just wondering why I suggested Risk—a game in which you can conquer the entire world if you're lucky with the dice. Mother knows I hate board games as much as she does.

The egg timer buzzes; the blueberry cake is ready.

"I'll be green!" Boy announces, passing us the other colors. Mother's yellow, Father is black, and of course he pushes the box with the pink counters toward me. Unfolding the board, he sets it in the middle of the dining table. Mother cuts the cake into equal portions and hands everyone a plate. Boy immediately stuffs a forkful of blueberry cake into his mouth. Father shuffles the territory cards as I discreetly study the colorful map of the world.

Six continents, forty-two territories. My eyes flit over names such as Peru, Siberia, Greenland, Scandinavia, Brazil. Congo, Central Europe, India, Western Australia, and Ontario.

"World domination or mission?" Father asks, dealing the cards. Boy takes the dice out of the box and rolls them across the board. "World domination!" he cries.

Mother picks up her territory cards. I look at mine, too. We begin dividing our armies between the territories. I'm lucky as I've got a counter in almost every territory in Australia. Easy to defend, if I cared about the game.

"That's not fair!" Boy says, pointing at my purple continent. "The cards weren't shuffled properly!"

Father takes a sip of his coffee.

"Where's Venezuela?" Boy asks, holding a green token. Mother points at a yellow country. "Right next to Peru." The board fills with colorful counters. "And where's China?" Boy scans the various continents. Father shows him the light-green territory to the east of the map.

"Western United States?"

"Here, on the left," I say. Boy has always had trouble finding his countries. It's no different today. That's what I was hoping. I've put almost all my armies out now, and I've only got two territory cards left. I stare at the board. Mother notices this and gives me a smile. "What are you looking for, Juno?"

My moment has arrived.

"Where's *Northland*?" I ask, leaning right across the board. "And *Southland*? I can't see them anywhere."

Father puts his cup back down on the saucer and adjusts his glasses. I look over at Mother, whose face has turned ashen.

"You're right, Juno!" Boy says, hurriedly searching the entire board. "Why aren't they on there?"

Springing up from the table, Mother piles the used plates on her forearm and stomps to the door. She stops just before leaving the room and turns around to Father. Her neck is scarlet. "Now do you understand why I wanted to toss this game on the fire?"

Mother disappears into the kitchen.

2

My name is Juno. I'm sixteen years old, and I've been living on this island for one hundred and forty-four months. Nobody knows that we've been hiding in the log cabin in the middle of the lake for these twelve years. The cabin behind the trees, behind thick trunks, heavy branches. No one knows, apart from the guards who brought us to the woods when I was still a little girl.

I love ducklings when they're newly hatched, buds in spring, globeflowers in my braided hair, blackberries as sweet as honey, the roar of elks at daybreak, the sparks that fly when birchwood is burning, the first snowflakes on my tongue.

And I like Boy, my little brother who secretly does those tasks I don't have the guts to do myself. Even though I'm much taller than him.

We lead a simple life here on the island. Every day is the same. In the mornings Mother gives us lessons in all those subjects we need for survival. Reading and writing, animals and nature, maths (I managed to persuade Father to let me do it, too), wound dressing, tracking, and domestic science. That means I've learned to knit and crochet, do the washing, wash the dishes, make a fire, and cook vegetable soup. I can also identify all the creatures and plants we share the island with. My brother, on the other hand, is only responsible for sourcing food on Sundays. Because I still can't bring myself to kill.

We have free time before supper. We can draw, pick wildflowers, read the books in the sitting room, listen to records, or play on the big rock down by the shore. Boy and I have invented dozens of games. Although lately he can be a bit annoying sometimes, we play every day. Apart from on Mondays, when it's strictly forbidden.

Boy picks up a stone and hits the head of the rudd again and again until the little fish starts to spasm. One last blow and the eyes go glassy. Boy intently takes the kitchen knife, stabs at the heart, and lets the rudd bleed. Short and painless, like we learned. It's the only way to survive on the island. Once a month, when the full moon stands high above the woods, Father is allowed to row over to the other side of the lake and buy essentials from the guards' village. Like flour, sugar, eggs, milk, and coffee beans.

I look at Boy. My brother grins, removes the hook from the fish's mouth and drops our catch into the plastic bucket with the trout. My beloved beach bucket with the picture of a mouse in a spotted summer dress.

My only memento of our flight from Southland.

I cast the line out again. We need one more rudd for the patties that Mother will make us for supper.

"Why did you do that?" Boy asks, breaking the silence. "Because of you, we didn't have our Sunday game."

"Risk is a silly game," I say, because I can't think of a better answer at the moment. In truth I've been feeling bad all afternoon because I know how much my brother was looking forward to Sunday. "Anyway, Mother calmed down again."

"But now we've got to wait another whole week!"

On the other side of the lake, in the shadows of the spruce wood, I detect a movement: two deer trotting through the undergrowth. Boy notices the animals, too. We watch them lift their heads and prick up their ears, ready to flee. For a brief moment, they are motionless, like in an oil painting. Then they peer over as if able to smell us.

Boy throws a stone into the water. At once the deer gallop away and disappear into the thicket.

He turns to me. "I've been thinking, Juno. It's something I've been considering for a long time. When Mother and Father are asleep, I'm going to row over there. Tonight."

"Are you mad?" I whisper. "You'll put us all in danger!"

"But you want to see what is on the other shore, too."

"No, I don't!"

Boy narrows his eyes and checks my right forefinger. "What about that drawing under your mattress?"

I clench my fist. He must have found the picture I drew yesterday afternoon on the big rock. Of houses towering into the clouds where a silver bird circles above a sea of sun umbrellas sprouting out of the sand like striped mushrooms and children play in the water.

I didn't draw any trees.

"I've been watching you, Juno," Boy says, moving closer and wagging his finger in my face. Then he puts the finger on my lips. "You're lying!" My nostrils are filled with a metallic fishy smell. "Say one word about my plan, and I'll show Father your picture."

I'd love to tell him that I'm not going to be blackmailed by a twelve-year-old, because the commandments are for our own safety, but my thoughts are disrupted by the wail of the sirens.

Boy yelps. I drop the rod, leap up, grab my brother's arm, and run with him through the vegetable garden. Past the tall loudspeaker masts, and we're almost at the house. The shrill cry of the warning sirens pierces my ears. I trip over the handle of a shovel. Boy pulls me back to my feet. Mother is waiting for us in the doorway, her eyes wide open, clapping her hands. "Come on, children. Quick!"

We race into the hallway as the front door slams shut behind us. Mother bolts it and follows us into the kitchen. Father has pushed the dining table to one side and rolled back the carpet.

A gaping hole in the floor.

Boy climbs in first, then Mother and Father go down. I take a step toward the trapdoor.

"For God's sake, Juno! What are you waiting for?" Father barks.

My heart is hammering like a hungry woodpecker. I move closer to the hole in the ground. Heat surges through my body. I wipe my finger on my dress, put my left foot on the ladder. Then my right.

"Come on; hurry up!"

Grabbing the sides of the ladder with both hands, I climb down. A cool draft wafts over my legs. I keep going until the tips of my toes feel the ground. Father squeezes past me and closes the heavy wooden door above us. The cold in our dungeon wraps itself around me like an invisible cloak.

"Turn the light on, please!" I whisper, as I hear Father lock the trapdoor with the metal bolt.

"Sit beside me, Juno," Mother says. I follow her voice from the other end of the room. She takes my hand and sits me on her lap. I cuddle up to her bodily warmth. I'd really like to crawl deep inside her, back inside her belly.

"Secured!" Father calls out. The click of a light switch comes as a huge relief. The bulb flickers on. A tear on Mother's cheek.

"Are they going to kill us?" Boy stammers. He's snuck into the corner of the safe room, his arms around his legs.

"We have to be quiet," Father whispers, looking up at the trapdoor. "Four strangers, dressed in black. They're already on the lake." Father picks up the rifle from the wall mount and wanders to the middle of the cellar where he sits on the armchair they discarded from the living room. The green checkered one we used to sit on when Mother read me *Thumbelina* in front of a crackling fire on those first few nights when I couldn't get to sleep.

Father gives me a nod. I understand what he's trying to say. I creep over to Boy and pick him up. Boy is shaking all over.

Mother gets up and goes over to the shelves that run the length of the wall and which are filled with the most essential supplies. More than fifty tins, a basket of fresh apples and pears, five bottles of high-percentage alcohol, three sacks of potatoes, a box of long candles, matches, jam jars of soused fish, a gas cooker, and fifteen canisters of water. Our survival rations for two weeks. Mother takes the first aid box off the shelf and sits on the floor beside us.

"What did we learn, children?" She unfastens the clasp on the green plastic box. "What do we have to do if there's no way out?"

"So they can't torture you?" Father says, looking again up at the bolted trapdoor. He takes a bullet out of his trouser pocket and loads it into the rifle.

"Many years ago your father took on a very heavy burden when he testified in front of the tribunal. He opted to tell the truth. And in doing so put justice above the welfare of his family." Mother flips open the lid, opens a packet of compresses, and cuts a square of material with a pair of scissors. "It was through Father's testimony alone that the most dangerous villains of Southland were arrested and thrown into prison for decades." Mother wipes the tears from her eyes with the cloth. "That's why they're searching for us all over the world."

"To take revenge." Father cocks the rifle. "On me and my family."

"But the guards of Northland are still protecting us, aren't they?" Boy asks, taking hold of my hand. His fingers are cold and clammy. I squeeze them gently and imagine bright, warm light flooding my body.

"Of course," Mother replies, stroking his hair.

"Why are they not coming, then?"

"We live too far out," I reply. "It takes the guards hours to get to us from the village."

"Can they hear our sirens so far away?"

"The alarm is just for us," I say. Sometimes Boy still behaves like a little child. I give his hand a firmer squeeze. "So that we all go to the safe room. You know that."

"Father has switched the sirens off now," Mother says, reaching into the first aid box again. Only now do I realize how silent it is.

"Don't worry, children," she whispers, pushing a number of ointments, syringes, and bandages to one side. "Father will protect us until we're rescued." She hesitates for a moment. Her hands tremble as she pulls out the long tube of pills. "Because we love you more than anything on earth."

"If I don't survive the attack or they try to get to you in the safe room," Father says, adjusting his glasses and looking up at the ceiling again, "you know what to do to protect yourselves, don't you?"

"Juno and I take the comfort pills," Boy says.

My heart leaps for joy. This is the moment I look forward to most.

"Correct." Mother unscrews the cap. Boy and I put out our palms. Only one pill each. I'd love to stuff it straight in my mouth; the pill that's meant to soothe our souls tastes sweeter than the ripest cherries.

Then we wait. Listen to the silence. Wait for the front door to be smashed in. Or a window. I breathe through my mouth. Count to ten. Mother dabs the bead of sweat on my brow with the piece of lint. Nobody says a word. Father checks his watch. I close my eyes and concentrate on every sound. Hear my heart pounding in my chest. I can even feel my pulse in my ears. Boy pulls his legs up more tightly to his body and leans his head on my shoulder. I can feel his hot breath on my arm. A strange rustling. A few meters above us. Were those footsteps in the kitchen? Have the strangers reached our island already? I stare upward, look at the beams that Father fixed to the wall with metal screws. It took him almost half a year to construct our safe room. Now it's full of spiderwebs. Fine sand trickles down onto us. I scrunch up my eyes and rub the dust from my lids. When I open them again, I can see white dots floating in the room. Like dancing elves, I think, come to protect us.

"I'm so proud of you," Father says, slapping his thigh. "Brilliant, as ever." He stands up from the armchair. "That was just a drill. Don't worry children, no strangers are coming to get us." Father hangs the rifle back up on the wall. "You did that so well!"

Boy breathes a sigh of relief and lets go of my hand. "I knew it all along!" I don't believe him. Even though I'd also hoped that it was just a practice, too. Without warning, like we have every year. But Mother's tears unsettled me; they were genuine.

"Can we still have this?" I ask, squinting at the amber-colored pill in my hand. Mother nods. I'm just about to put it in my mouth when Father interrupts us. "First I want to hear the seven commandments again."

On cue, Boy and I recite the commandments. We could do it in our sleep.

"We have to hide when Uncle Ole comes."

"We must never lie."

"No one's allowed to enter Father's library," Boy says, sneering at me. I only took a few old photo albums and Mother's favorite novel off the shelves. The one with the beautiful woman on the cover, in a tight embrace with a dark-haired man. I'd just sat at the desk and read the first chapter of *Juliette, or The Love of My Life*, when Father suddenly appeared behind me. I'd felt so embarrassed, caught red-handed. A page of the book must have gotten torn. Mother was so angry about this that we've been forbidden from going into Father's study ever since. Even though I still think that's unfair. It was only a tiny rip.

"When we hear the siren, we have to go to the safe room straightaway. No matter what we're doing."

"We mustn't eat any berries we're not sure of," I say, remembering the time when Boy was in bed for three days with a fever and cramps. For security reasons, we couldn't call a doctor from the village, so we prayed to God every night for his survival. The fifth commandment was introduced when Boy got better.

"We must always kill quickly and painlessly."

"And the seventh and most important rule: We're not allowed to leave our island without Mother's or Father's permission," I say, glancing over at Boy. "Otherwise, both of us will be punished."

"To make sure we look after each other," Boy snarls back.

"Well done, well done." Father is satisfied. We stuff the comfort pills in our mouths. I close my eyes and let the fruity jelly mixture of ripe wild strawberries, elderflower, cherries, and sour cranberries linger on my tongue before swallowing the fat, tasteless pill hidden in its sugary coating.

I wish we had a drill like this every week.

After supper I lie in bed, staring at the ceiling. My mind is churning; I can't help thinking of my brother. The ticking of the alarm clock makes me jittery. I turn over to my bedside table where I can see the clock, my lucky black stone, Father's carved elk, and a vase of wildflowers. My eye focuses on the second hand. It's half past eleven. Is Boy really planning to break one of the commandments tonight and row over to the other side?

Pushing the duvet aside, I put on my slippers. The door squeaks when I open it and go out onto the upstairs landing. Boy's room is at the end of the corridor, right beside the bathroom. I creep over to his door. The wooden floor creaks beneath my feet. If Father wakes up and finds me here, I'll just dart into the bathroom. I carefully push Boy's door and go in. It smells of damp pine needles and twinflowers. A breath of wind caresses my face; I stare at the open paned window. The hoot of a small owl echoes through the night: an alarm call. Hopping over to the window, I scan the shore of the lake. The moonlight dances on the water like a finely woven carpet of diamonds. My eyes wander to the big rock. And then I see it. Father's boat, still beside our jetty. Relieved, I turn around to Boy's bed.

He's asleep. In my panic I hadn't noticed him. I close the window and kneel by his bed. Putting my hands together I hurriedly mumble an "Our Father" and thank God that my brother hasn't left me alone on the island. I stand up again and pull the duvet over his shoulders. For a moment I watch him as he sleeps. Even though we don't look much alike, we both share the same wish.

Very soon, my little brother, the two of us will embark on our adventure and discover the forbidden world out there. I promise you this.

However many strangers are lying in wait for us.

3

Today is Monday. Uncle Ole day. I wolf down a large bowl of warm porridge. Last time, he stayed at our house for two hours, and I'd forgotten to have breakfast. Boy and I waited impatiently in our hiding place; my tummy was growling like a rabid wildcat. Uncle Ole almost noticed us.

I was still playing with dollies when the old man first turned up on our island in his black floppy hat and raincoat. I vividly recall standing by the window, watching in fascination as the little motorboat suddenly appeared out of the fog. Mother tore me away from the window and hurried me into the bedroom, where we hid for hours in the wardrobe. Now I can understand Mother's distress, her fear. She couldn't have known that Uncle Ole was a guard, not a stranger. Ever since that day, Uncle Ole has crossed the lake every Monday to bring us post and newspapers.

I hurry to finish the last mouthful, rinse the bowl clean, and put it back in the cupboard.

"Are you going to come to the rock with me?" I whisper to Boy, who's lying on the sofa and leafing through a nature book.

"But Uncle Ole will be here any moment," Boy replies without looking up. "The first commandment?"

"Just for a bit," I say, going over to him. "We'll be careful. Please, Boy!" He glances up from his book, and I raise my eyebrows. He can tell at once that there's something on my mind, and he shuts the book. We put on our shoes and go out into the garden. The air is moist and cool. The sun stands high above the woods, and drops of dew are still on the salad leaves in the vegetable patch. We run along the sandy path, through a copse, and then the big rock appears before us. It stands there all alone, as if a troll had forgotten it when playing ball. We clamber to the top of the rock and sit on the viewing ledge.

I gaze down at the brownish-black lake, our legs dangling several meters above the surface of the water. It's strange, but the lake doesn't look at all dangerous today. It seems enticing, almost magical.

A family of ducks quacks its way past us. I'd love to be in the water, too, and swim over to the other side, but we've never learned how to.

"Thanks for not going," I say, putting my hand on Boy's shoulder. "Last night."

Boy bows his head. "It was that silly alarm's fault. It scared me. Anyway, leaving the island's against the seven commandments. I didn't want you to get punished because of me. It was a stupid idea."

"No," I say, tossing a stone into the water that's as heavy as the one in my stomach. "You were right, Boy. About the drawing under my bed, what you guessed."

He raises his head.

"I want to get off the island, too. At least for a day."

"Since when?"

"Sometimes I have these strange dreams. About tall houses and people beneath colorful umbrellas, children playing on the beach. It feels like a memory. Of back in Southland. Our island, that can't be all there is, can it, Boy?"

"Is that why you ruined our Sunday game?"

"Haven't you also wondered why Northland and Southland aren't marked on the board?"

Boy stares pensively at the water. All of a sudden, he looks older, more mature. Not like a twelve-year-old. "Do you think the territories Ontario and Australia really exist?"

"I'd like to find out, at least."

"What if the strangers catch you?"

"We'll just have to be careful."

"We? Juno, we can't run away from here," Boy hisses, ripping a bunch of grass from a crack in the rock. "The guards have forbidden it. Anyway, Mother and Father would die of worry. And then they'd come looking for us, on the other side of the lake, all over Northland. Just imagine what the strangers would do to us when they caught us. Do you want to risk that?"

"We could write a letter promising Mother that we'd come back in the evening."

"Let's say your great idea with the letter works," Boy says, turning to me. "How do you think we're going to protect ourselves over there? With Father's rifle?"

I'd already considered this, but I immediately dismissed the plan because I don't know how to use it. "We'll find a way."

Suddenly I hear Uncle Ole, the clatter of his motorboat. He's only a few meters away.

"Shit! Down from the rock!" My pulse is racing. I hope he hasn't spotted us. We scramble down and run back to the house. "Why's he so early today?" I pant, as Boy overtakes me and soon vanishes into the spruces. My left leg is burning; I stop, exhausted, and look at my knee. It's bleeding. I must have cut it while getting off the rock. "Wait for me, Boy!"

Bracing my arms on my thighs, I take a couple of deep breaths. It's hurting more. When I turn around, I get a shock. Uncle Ole's boat is moored at the jetty; he must be on the island already and making his way toward our cabin. He can't have gotten very far yet, thank goodness. Uncle Ole uses a walking stick, as he's got back problems. That's what Father told us. All the same, I can't just walk in the front door now or he'll see me.

Heading for the back door that leads to our pantry, I leap over a pile of firewood and run as fast as I can. I hear the front door opening and Father's angry voice. Boy is getting a severe telling off for being outside, although it was all my fault. I get to the back of the house and lean against the wall. Taking a deep breath, I slide to the ground. A stone digs into the palm of my hand; I wince. If I hurry, I'll just be able to get inside in time.

I duck as I sneak beneath the white windows. My kneecap feels like it's on fire. After a few meters, I'm by the back door. Tentatively I stand upright again and peer through the kitchen window. I can see Father help Uncle Ole sit on a chair, while Mother's at the sink getting him a glass of water. I'm too late. All I can do is wait here by the back door. Wait, watch, and listen. I never had the chance to watch Uncle Ole up close until now.

"*God morgon*. You're the first ones on my itinerary today," I hear Uncle Ole's muffled voice say through the glass pane as he clumsily drops onto the chair. "*Sovit gott?*"

"Yes, *tack*."

"I thought the letter was important."

"Thanks, Ole. We've been waiting for it for ages." Father takes the blue envelope and puts it with his weekly newspaper. "If we'd known you were coming earlier, you'd have had a cup of fresh coffee."

"Please don't go to any trouble."

"How's the back? Still sensitive to the weather?" Mother asks, placing the glass of water on the table.

"Oh, I grew up in this climate. You get used to it," he says with a chuckle, then takes a sip of water. "It's like life." Uncle Ole stares out of the window. "Sun one day, rain the next." He looks me straight in the eye for what feels like an eternity. In horror I drop to the ground and dive into a bunch of nettles. My upper arms start itching at once.

I hear a glass smash on the kitchen floor.

"Are you alright, Ole?" Mother asks.

"What happened?" Father sounds concerned, too.

"Don't move, I'll have it swept up in a jiffy. I wouldn't want you to cut yourself." A cupboard door is opened, then I hear the scrape of a brush as Mother sweeps the shards into a dustpan.

"*Herregud!* Who is that girl?" I hear Uncle Ole say through the wooden wall. My heart stops beating. "There was a child at the window just now!"

A brief silence before Father gives a nervous laugh. "A girl? You must be seeing things. How could a child get onto our island?"

"A girl with long hair."

"You must be mistaken, Ole. Here, on our island?" Mother says, agreeing with Father. "You haven't got your glasses on."

"I only need them for reading. I've got eyes like a hawk. Even though I'm over seventy."

"Well, I didn't see anything at the window. It must have been an optical illusion, a reflection."

"Or a bird flying past."

For a moment Uncle Ole says nothing. Please, please, dear God, he's got to believe he was mistaken.

I hear a relieved laugh. "I expect you're right. At my age I am beginning to see ghosts. They're just waiting to come and get me." Now Father's laughing, too. I offer a prayer of thanks up to heaven. A chair is pushed back. A painful groan as Uncle Ole gets to his feet. "I'm really sorry about the breakage. I'll replace the glass, of course."

"Are you going already?"

"Yes, I'm afraid so. My next stop is the Sjöberg family. See you next Monday."

They leave the kitchen. I scratch my arms, which are now covered in red blisters. At least my knee has stopped bleeding. I creep around the corner of the house and hear the front door open. Like a capuchin monkey out of Boy's nature book, I scurry on all fours beneath the windows before throwing myself flat on my tummy a few meters from our front door. Uncle Ole hobbles down the ramshackle wooden steps, which creak with every movement.

"...possible. I really miss her," Uncle Ole says. "Since she moved away with her parents." He seems different, sad. "*Å andra sidan*, you're absolutely right. Maybe I should just pick up the phone, call my granddaughter and get her to come and visit for the weekend." I leap between two birch trees.

"Do that. And thanks for the post." Father offers Uncle Ole his hand. "See you next Monday, Ole."

The old man shakes it, raises his walking stick as a parting gesture, and limps hurriedly down to the jetty. A family of wild geese flies over our heads.

When Uncle Ole is out of earshot, Father spins around to Mother and says, "Christ! He must have seen Juno!"

"Thank goodness you were able to convince him it was just his imagination," Mother says. "And luckily it reminded him of his granddaughter."

"Granddaughter?" Father's voice is quaking. "Come off it, Ole doesn't even have children!"

There's going to be big trouble, is the thought that shoots through my head. I'll be confined to my room. If not worse.

"No, he lied to us." Father adjusts his glasses. "What if he spreads the word that there's a child on our island?" Father gives Ole one last wave before shoving Mother into the house. The front door slams behind them.

My heart is thumping. Why didn't I just stay in my hiding place? Father's right. My curiosity has put us all in serious danger. There's a chance that Ole will be captured by the strangers on his way back to the village. And what if he tells them about me? Then they'll come here and kill the lot of us. I've got to do something right now; there's no time to lose. I rack my brains, as I scratch all the stings on my arm. Maybe if I begged Uncle Ole not to tell anyone about me, I could make up for my mistake somehow. He's got to understand what's at stake. He is the only one who can make this better. I've barely thought this through to its conclusion before I'm already dashing down to the lake.

Uncle Ole is untying his boat when I get to the shore. "Uncle Ole!"

The old man drops the rope and turns around to me in astonishment. He stares at me, wide-eyed, as if he'd just spotted a fairy on a flower.

"I know you saw me at the kitchen window. But you mustn't tell anyone about me!" I take a few steps toward him. "Please, Uncle Ole!"

Removing his floppy hat, he wipes his brow with his hand, which is wrinkled and gray. Veins bulge through his skin. He narrows his eyes, peers up at our log cabin, then back at me. Uncle Ole appears older than I thought he was. He looks me up and down, his mouth slightly open. Like a lethargic, ancient, giant tortoise, I think, staring at the thin threads of saliva stuck to his lips. His few remaining teeth are stubby and yellow. "Who are you?" he eventually asks, spluttering as he sits on the edge of the boat. A sour, rotten smell drifts into my nostrils. "Your face. It looks somehow familiar."

"Juno," I answer curtly. "Like the goddess."

"How did you get onto this island, my girl?"

"I live here. With my parents."

"So why have I never seen you before?"

I'm frantically debating whether I ought to let him in on our family secret, which has protected us from the strangers all these years. But I don't have any choice. "You mustn't tell anyone that we live on the island. Otherwise they'll kill us all."

"Who's going to kill you?"

"They'll pay money to the person who finds us."

"*Jösses!* Is there a bounty on your heads?" Uncle Ole asks in surprise, raising his bushy eyebrows. "How much is it?"

I don't understand what he means by *bounty*. But I distinctly remember Mother telling us in our safe room last year that the strangers had promised all the residents of the village a wooden chest full of gold coins if they revealed our hiding place. "The guards brought us here many years ago. Because Father testified against the strangers in front of the tribunal. Back in Southland."

"Sørlandet? Do you mean the region in southern Norway?" Uncle Ole says, fixing his eyes on our log cabin again. He seems confused.

I'm puzzled, too, and I still don't understand what he's talking about. "No, I mean where the beach is. And the sea."

"Here in Sweden?"

"Argentina." The words just come out. It's the southernmost country I can remember on the board. "Or maybe South Africa."

Uncle Ole frowns. He doesn't believe me. I need to put all my eggs in one basket. "Father says we're living here under a witness protection screen or something like that. I can't remember the right term." As proof I hold my right forefinger up to his face. It doesn't budge one millimeter. "I'm not lying. Ever since I was a little girl, we've been hiding on this island in Northland. From the strangers. But you're not one of those, are you?"

"Witness protection scheme?" Uncle Ole mutters. "And there's a big reward for you, is that right?"

"Yes, lots and lots of gold coins."

Uncle Ole smiles at me. Finally he appears to have understood. I breathe a sigh of relief. Once again Uncle Ole looks up at our house while he feels in his coat pocket and takes out a slim object. The black front of this little case shines like the surface of the lake at night.

"Don't worry, my girl. I won't tell anyone about you," Uncle Ole says, putting his thumb on the device, which beeps. "Promise." Then he holds the strange thing up to my face.

"What's that?"

"Please don't smile," Uncle Ole says. But it's really hard not to, seeing as there's now a big weight off my mind, a weight as big as our rock. I've managed to save our family in the nick of time.

But I try. I close my eyes, think of Mother and Father, who will no doubt be very proud of me, take a deep breath, and attempt to relax the corners of my mouth, which are pulling upward with great force. When I open my eyes again, I'm blinded by a harsh light.

"Thanks," Uncle Ole says, putting the little case back in his coat pocket and doing up the zip.

He's not smiling anymore now; the jollity seems to have ebbed from his face.

He pushes the boat into the water, gets in, and sits in the middle of the wooden bench. The boat rocks perilously from side to side. "You must never tell your parents we had this chat," Uncle Ole warns me, starting the engine. "Never. Do you understand, Juno?" He stares at me with icy eyes. "Otherwise I'll betray the lot of you. You and all your family."

I feel sick.

4

I lie on my bed, waiting for breakfast, which Mother's going to leave outside my door. My tummy is grumbling.

It's Tuesday, and I'm confined to my room for two days. It's my punishment from Father, because I didn't make it to my hiding place in time. Mother was so furious she wanted to make it a whole week. I wanted to tell her she needn't worry and that I sorted everything out like a grown woman. And so long as I keep my mouth shut—which I'm going to—Uncle Ole won't give us away. He promised.

Never lie.

The seven commandments will end up applying throughout Northland, I think, and shuffle to the window, feeling relieved. I peer down into the garden, at the freshly cut lawn outside our front door. Right beside it, between the two birches that are as tall as a house, Father has planted the vegetable patch: salad, celery, potatoes, tomatoes, herbs, and berries.

Mother is kneeling in front of it with a raffia basket, picking strawberries. Probably to add some sweetness to my porridge. I knock at the window, but Mother doesn't seem to hear me. I knock harder. She turns around and looks up at me blankly. I wave and give her a smile, but she doesn't return my greeting and goes back to picking berries.

Disappointed, I look out to the other side of the lake. The sun is high above the pine woods, flooding my entire bedroom with light. I lean my head against the warm glass of the window. Being confined to your room is so boring. But Mother is right; it's what I deserve. I stroke the pane of glass with my finger and trace the outline of the big rock. Why am I always so inquisitive? Although *always* isn't quite right. It's only the last few weeks that I've felt this inexplicable urge to find out everything about the unfamiliar world beyond our island. I can't say what triggered this. Maybe the recurring dreams of tower-like houses, strange silver birds in the sky, girls laughing in the water. But perhaps I've just grown up. Because to my surprise, I'm beginning to question things in life. Like Mother's educational methods, which supposedly are for our protection. By now I can decide for myself what's good for me and what isn't. After all I *am* sixteen. And it's high time I had some answers about Northland and Southland.

And about boys. I don't mean my little brother—God forbid—but someone a bit mysterious like Richard Blackwood, the young, cute-looking man from Mother's *Juliette* novel. I can't say where this sudden longing comes from, either; it makes me feel all giddy inside. It just appeared from nowhere.

Out of the corner of my eye I see a flock of birds passing me like a dark cloud. They circle the lake, above the big rock.

I freeze.

Our boat—it's gone! I'm seized by panic; I instinctively think of the telling off Father gave us yesterday when I came back in the house.

We'd never seen him so nasty before. Even Mother growled at us for not staying in our hiding place. Boy threw himself on the kitchen floor, crying over and over again that it wasn't his fault. But it was no use; he knows the score. If a commandment is broken, both children get punished. That's how we get better at looking out for each other. I still think it's unfair. And I felt sorry for Boy. In the past I would have just given in silently without complaining. But not yesterday.

I screamed at Father that it was all my fault and it was unfair my brother had to pay for my stupidity. Then Mother slapped me, something she'd never done before. I could see she was surprised at herself. But I just felt stronger, more in the right.

"It's all your fault!" I shouted defiantly. "If you'd just tell us how much longer we have to stay on this stupid island, we wouldn't be so curious!"

"What has got into you, Juno?"

"Up to your rooms. Both of you!"

I stroke my cheek and look down at the jetty. I wasn't imagining it. Our boat has gone. Boy must have escaped from the island last night, no question about it. Without me. Pursing my lips, I watch Mother put a handful of strawberries into the basket. She doesn't seem to have noticed yet. I hold my breath. Mother gets up, shakes the earth from her apron, and totters back to the house.

I can't help thinking of the punishment awaiting me if our seventh commandment is broken, the most important one. A shiver runs down my spine.

I don't want to go into the safe room.

But that's what's in store for me when they discover Boy has escaped. Feverishly I look around my room. I've got to do something. Maybe I should hide? In the wardrobe, beneath my bed? If Father thinks both children have escaped the island together, they won't look for me in my room. I'll just stick it out in my hiding place until Boy comes back.

I go over to the wardrobe, push to one side my wellies, sleeping bag, my old doll Mirabell, *Grimms' Fairy Tales*, and the painted cigar box where I keep all the treasures I've collected from the lake, climb onto the bottom shelf, and close the doors behind me. It instantly turns dark. Exhausted, I lean against the back of the wardrobe, pull my legs up to my chest, and try breathing through my nose as quietly as possible. It smells of fresh soap and stained wood. I need to calm down. I need to come up with a plan.

How will Mother react when she realizes I'm not in my room? Will she call for Father first or rush into my brother's room?

Something brushes my face, probably the thick green jumper with the reindeers on it that Mother knitted for my fourteenth birthday. When I push the itchy wool away, the clothes hanger grates on the metal rail above me. I lean forward and peer through the gap between the wardrobe doors. Specks of dust float in the shining sunlight. I screw up my eyes but can only make out the edge of my bed and part of my attic window. So, Juno, what's the plan? Mother could be on the landing any second now to bring me my porridge for breakfast.

I picture her unlocking the door and entering my empty room. The tray slides from her hands and the bowl smashes on the floor as she legs it out of the room and calls for Father. They'll wonder how I could have escaped from the locked room. And then Father will point to the open window, the only logical way for me to escape. My heart misses a beat.

The window! It's shut.

I kick open the wardrobe doors with both feet, scramble out, and dart to the other end of the room. Within seconds I've undone the little metal window lock and opened the window. Cool air strokes my hot cheeks. I take a deep breath. Why didn't I think of it earlier? I bite my lower lip in irritation.

A sheet comes to mind—I have to fasten some kind of rope to the frame and dangle it out of the window to make my escape look convincing.

In truth I'm not one for spontaneous decisions; I'm certain that's how most mistakes are made. Father says that with my mathematical ability I'm bound to construct complex machines when I'm older. Or bridges and log cabins. He is so impressed he doesn't mind teaching me mathematics anymore.

The thing is, I don't like surprises. Not even on my birthday. By now Mother and Father have accepted this quirk of mine and they give me my presents unwrapped. Ever since my thirteenth birthday. I don't know why, but it gives me a feeling of security.

I hear a key in the lock and turn around. The handle angles down. Mother comes into my bedroom, holding a tray.

"What are you doing?"

"Just getting some fresh air," I reply quickly, before shutting the window again and leaping onto my mattress. I pray Mother doesn't look down at the lake and see the empty jetty. She comes over to me and puts the tray on my bedside table.

"Listen, Juno," Mother says, sitting on my bed. "I'm really sorry. I didn't mean to hit you." She strokes my head. "I was just worried. Do you understand?"

Surprised, I hesitate for a moment. Mother has never apologized to me before, or talked about feelings.

"And I didn't mean to be wicked," I say, wrapping my arms around her and pulling her tightly toward me.

The two of us weep. It feels good.

After a while Mother frees herself from our embrace and looks me in the eye. "Is something troubling you, Juno? You know you can tell me anything. I mean, I am your mother."

I think about my conversation with Uncle Ole at the shore. And about the missing boat. There's so much I'd like to say to Mother. But I'd be severely punished for it all.

"OK, then," Mother says. "I've picked you some strawberries. I know how much you love them." She gives me a friendly smile and hands me the bowl. "Have we made up now?"

"Boy's gone."

"What?"

"By boat," I say, pointing at the window.

"That's impossible." Mother looks at my right forefinger. It's not moving. "Your brother's in his room. The door's locked."

She gets up and goes over to the window. There's going to be big trouble, now. But instead she turns around and smiles. "Father rowed over to the other side yesterday, Juno. Right after Uncle Ole left. He's doing our monthly shopping in the village. Had you forgotten?"

"Full moon," I say softly, regretting that I didn't think before opening my mouth.

"I'm expecting him back very soon. Maybe this time he'll even bring us..." Mother pauses and stares motionless out of the window. "Tell me, Juno. What makes you think that Boy wants to leave the island?"

I press my fingernails into the heels of my hand so hard that it hurts. "Because of yesterday evening," I blurt out.

"Nonsense," Mother says brusquely, drawing the curtains. A warm, orange light veils the walls, my wardrobe, the stripy rug, the bedside table, and our faces. Mother sits back down on the bed. "Your brother would never take such a risk."

But I would, I think. Mother sighs as if she could read my mind. I sink my chin onto my chest and put my hands in my lap. Please, God, don't let her ask any more questions.

"Juno, look at me," Mother says, grabbing my right forefinger and squeezing her hand around it. "You children aren't planning to row to the other side, are you?"

I don't reply. She squeezes harder and I can feel the blood throbbing in my finger.

"No, Mother."

"I remember when I was your age, Juno. At fifteen I believed I was grown up." She shifts closer. "And I was the only person who knew how the big, wide world worked. That's why I wanted to explore it. But I was just a silly little girl."

I concentrate on my finger that's stuck in Mother's hand like a vice. It hurts.

"You're growing wings, my girl. But that's very dangerous for our family, do you understand? I've always feared this moment. We've only got one boat. If one of you rows over there, Father will never get off the island again. He can't come looking for you. He can't save you if the strangers..." She falters and lets go of my finger. "I'd die of worry thinking that something might happen to you out there." Mother grabs her throat. "Is that what you want?"

I hate lying.

But then I clench my fist.

5

Mother is washing the blood out of Father's shirt. We stand huddled around the sink in the kitchen, watching her scrub the material with soap in a circular motion. But like my desire to leave the island, the stains won't go away. And this pantomime that Mother's been putting on for us since breakfast isn't going to change that one bit.

"The strangers injured him badly," she explains, holding the shirt beneath the tap. "It took every ounce of Father's strength to get away. He escaped by a whisker."

"I hope they didn't follow him to the island," Boy says, chewing his fingernails as if they were carrot sticks. "They don't know where we live, do they?"

I want to tell my brother not to worry. That Mother's just trying to scare us. Because that's what I reckon. She must have guessed we're toying with the idea of leaving the island. My finger must have given it away. And because keeping us locked up in our rooms doesn't seem to be able to quell our longing, she had to come up with this dreadful hoax to make us believe that Father was attacked on his way back from the village. By the strangers. As expected, Boy's fallen for it. But I'm not twelve anymore. So I play along, shifting my weight from one foot to the other, acting the part of the frightened girl. Even though I'm sure it's varnish she's washing out of Father's shirt. It's the same color as the tool shed behind our house. I know that fresh blood is lighter. Fish's blood is, at least.

"Father knows the woods like the back of his hand. He hid behind a big tree stump until the strangers went away," Mother says, rubbing harder with the soap.

"Is that why he came back so late last night?"

"Your father was scared to death," Mother says, dropping the shirt into the sink and inserting a plug. She turns on the tap. "He couldn't just row back to the island. That would have led the strangers straight to us."

I look at my brother and see the fear in his eyes. He grabs Mother's arm. "So now they're on the other side, looking for us?"

"Yes. We think they're still in the woods."

Smart move, I think. They want to stop us from rowing across the lake. I'm amazed by my reasoning. A few days ago I would have been just as frightened as Boy. Like a little girl. But I'm not a little girl anymore. I ask questions and find solutions. After meeting Uncle Ole I suddenly feel more mature, braver. I'd explained the problem like a grown-up woman and acted on the spur of the moment. I'd love to tell Mother about my heroism; then she could stop this ludicrous scrubbing.

"This isn't a drill, Juno."

"Of course it isn't, Mother," I say, crossing my hands behind my back. "We'd have had to stay in our rooms, otherwise."

"Indeed," Mother says, turning off the tap. "It's vital you

understand that." She points at the half-filled sink. Father's shirt rises like a solitary island from the rusty-colored water. "This is more important than being confined to your rooms."

"Yes, Mother."

"How is Father?" Boy asks, looking at the wooden stairs that lead up to the bedrooms.

"He needs peace and quiet right now. Please don't disturb him."

"Will his wounds heal?"

"I had to stitch them," Mother says. "But Father's over the worst. He'll be back on his feet in a few days."

"I'm going to draw him a picture," Boy says. "Of our family."

"He'll be delighted with that," Mother says, stroking my brother's cheek.

"And I'm going to pick Father some flowers," I hurriedly add. It's my chance to finally get out into the garden. Maybe even down to the lake. "May I?" I curtsey.

Mother nods. Then she turns back to the sink and gets going on the shirt again. Boy and I exchange glances then zip out of the kitchen, each of us with a different goal. But before going out, I pop into the sitting room and make for the chair where Father reads his weekly paper on Mondays. Behind this, on the narrow windowsill, I see them, between the dragon tree, yuccas, and mistletoe cactus. Always at hand. I grab the binoculars and slip out into the garden. I just can't take their lies anymore. I need to find a way to get off this island as quickly as possible.

The bunch of wildflowers lies on the rock in front of me. I've put my right leg on the prickly stems to stop them from being blown away.

There's no time to pick new ones; Mother would get suspicious if I came back so late. After all, I didn't run down to the shore because of the flowers.

I take hold of Father's binoculars that are dangling around my neck and look through them at the other side of the lake. I feel giddy at once. It's all blurry, milky green. Everything is spinning. My body starts to sway; I snatch the binoculars from my eyes. Bracing myself on the rock, I stare at my feet in their red sandals that are dangling five meters above the dark surface of the water.

When my eyes are better, I grab the binoculars again. They feel heavy in my hand. But before I take another look, I turn the little knob between the eyepieces. This is how blind Father must be when he's misplaced his glasses, I think, adjusting the focus ring all the way.

I can make out every single leaf on the birch tree, and even the white-ringed bark far away on the other side of the lake. I move the binoculars to the left and focus on the dense pine wood. A thin shaft of sunlight squeezes through the trees, falling onto moss-covered crevices and weather-beaten tree stumps. I can even see a hedgehog mushroom at the foot of a pine tree. And then, only a few centimeters to the right, I finally spot it: Uncle Ole's narrow track through the woods. The path to the village—my path to freedom.

Everything looks so close, as if I could touch it.

I've decided on my plan. I'm going to row to the other side this week. Secretly, when Mother and Father are asleep. I'll wake Boy, and together we'll explore a new world out there. Where the trees are greener, the houses bigger, and the people more honest. Mother's treated me like a little child for long enough, something that's clearer with every passing day. But I don't want to hear any more fairy tales about the wicked strangers who attacked Father. I need to experience the world for myself. I mean, I am sixteen. No longer a silly little girl, but a grown-up woman with my own wishes and desires. But Mother doesn't understand this. All that matters to her are obedience and punishment. When I'm with her I feel lonely and misunderstood. I'd scream at her if only I were braver.

I point the binoculars at our jetty and watch Father's rowing boat sway softly on the waves. Ever since Boy and I can remember we've been strictly forbidden from getting into the boat. Not even for fun. We could capsize and drown. So I don't know how it works.

I scan the boat for a hidden steering mechanism; using the binoculars I study every screw, every board. And suddenly I discover a shiny black patch on the floor, in the shadow of the front seats. A pool of water, maybe? I think. Does the boat have a leak? I wheel the knob slightly to the left. Now everything is blurred. I readjust it, but I still can't tell what liquid it is. At least not from up here on the big rock. I need to go down.

The bunch of flowers slips from my hand as I approach the boat. No doubt about it, that red shimmer isn't water. The dark patch must be blood. Father wouldn't pour dark paint into his beloved rowing boat just to stop us children from rowing to the other side. His shirt's different. That can be washed.

Anxiously I sit down on the edge of the boat, which immediately lurches forward, so I steady myself with my arms and legs, making the boat rock back and forth like a walnut shell. The water is up to my ankles. Bracing all my strength against the boat, I restore some sort of balance. Then I hear the metallic jangling behind me.

I turn around and see the chain wrapped around the back seat several times. In confusion my eyes follow every link of the chain. Over the edge of the boat, through the shallow water and to our jetty, where the chain is secured with a thick lock.

I laugh out loud even though I could howl. Not in despair, but because at this moment I realize everything is part of their wicked game. And I almost fell for it. The alleged blood on the shirt, the alleged blood in the rowing boat. I shake my head. The laughter has subsided. They might be able to scare my brother with this trick but not me. I'm not that gullible, and Mother knows it. No, for me Father has come up with an insurmountable obstacle: an iron chain.

Devastated, I trudge out of the water and drop onto the grass. The realization hits me like a thunderbolt. It's not the rowing boat they've put in chains, but me. I'm never going to leave this island.

A falcon is circling in the cloudless sky; I follow its graceful aerial display. What I'd give to be as free as that. I ought to be able to fly. Or swim, I think, as I sit up again and look across the lake to the other shore. Over there, only a few hundred meters away in the shadows of the tall trees, lies my future. But it's being denied to me by my own parents, something I realize so clearly, now.

I'm gripped by anger. What are a few days of confinement in my room against another fifteen years on this island? Exactly, it makes no difference. I've been a prisoner all my life, and I'll remain so unless I do something about it immediately.

Leaning forward, I undo the buckles on my sandals and toss my shoes into the grass beside me. Then I leap up and slip my summer dress over my head. It's time to act. Today I'm going to take my destiny in my hands and learn how to swim. Surely it can't be that hard.

A pleasant summer warmth envelops my skin. I take tentative steps toward the water. The lake is glistening so invitingly, as if trying to give me courage, but just a few meters out the surface looks terrifyingly dark. I plop my right foot into the brown water, then my left. The soft mud squidges beneath my feet. I venture a few more steps, deeper into the lake, until the water's up to my knees. A dragonfly darts elegantly past. Carefully I squat, feeling the cold creep up my bare legs like a second skin, over my tummy, my belly button, up to my breasts. I let myself float forward until the whole of my body is underwater. I thrash about with my arms and legs like a frog. I swallow water. Spluttering, I stand up again. It feels good to have ground safely beneath my feet again. Maybe this is easier than I thought. Taking a deep breath in and out, I squat again, splay my arms and start to swim.

I manage three strokes before going under.

6

I spend the next afternoon in the water and make it nearly halfway across the lake. I'm so proud of myself. Nobody has taught me, it's all my own work. Setting my fear aside I just plunged into the cold water. Swimming isn't that hard; why won't they let us learn how to do it? To ensure we spend our entire lives on this island, I think, angrily spreading out my arms and using all my strength to push myself through the water, kicking wildly with my feet. I don't feel at all cold anymore. After a few strokes I turn around until I reach the safety of our shore.

I pick up the towel and dry myself. Nervously I glance in the direction of our cabin, which lies hidden behind the pine copse. I put on the blue stripy dress and my sandals. Nobody saw me secretly practicing my swimming, I hope, although it would be extremely unlikely in this forbidding place. That's why I chose it. Only rarely does anyone in my family come down this way. I used to be afraid of this place, but I'm not anymore. For most of the day the tall, dense trees keep the shore in the dark. Everywhere there are large, moss-covered stones and trees that have fallen into the reeds. A young wagtail hops around, chirruping.

Now I feel cold; my body is shivering. I examine my crinkled fingertips. There must be no signs that I was in the lake; I need to wait until the ends of my hair are dry. But it might take a while, as the sun almost never makes an appearance in this spot.

All of a sudden I hear a noise above me. I look up and follow the unfamiliar hum a few meters above me in the sky. It's a strange black creature—what is it? I've never seen this sort of bird on the island before. Maybe it's a huge insect, I wonder; after all it has four slim wings, all pointing outwards. That would explain the shrill humming, like a swarm of angry bees.

Hopefully it doesn't sting.

In panic I throw the towel over my head and beg God to make the thing above me go away.

I wait, trying to remain perfectly still. But without success; my entire body starts to tremble, as if Mother were shaking me furiously. I hold my breath. The noise is coming closer. I stiffen; the strange creature must have seen me! Its hissing gets more aggressive, as if it might pounce on me at any moment. Now it's deafeningly loud, and I sense it's only a few centimeters above my head.

I flail the towel wildly around my head to try to repel the insect and start running. Don't look back, Juno, faster! Past the two birch trees, through the dark pine copse, past my older sister's grave, then just a few more paces to the well. I don't dare turn around as I pass the old tool shed, vault the currant bushes, and then I'm at the back door to our cabin.

"For heaven's sake, Juno!" Mother says, her arms on her hips when I come racing into the kitchen. "Where were you?"

"Down by the lake."

"Why is your hair wet?"

"I fell into the water," I stammer. My right index finger starts to tingle. "I didn't mean to. I got a fright."

"What happened?" She sounds concerned. "Juno, you could have drowned!"

"There was this huge insect. It was going to sting me," I splutter. "By the grave."

She looks at me skeptically, then grabs my right wrist and pulls the hand up to her face to check. "An insect? What sort of insect?"

"A big, black beetle, I think. With four wings," I say truthfully. "It even hissed."

"Hissed?" Mother says, sounding puzzled. She's still holding my finger up to her eyes; it's as stiff as a pencil. "It might have been a pine chafer. They make noises when they feel threatened." Mother frowns pensively. "But they're very rare."

I've never heard of a bug that can hiss before, but Mother must know. She used to be a biologist back in Southland. That's why there are so many nature books in our house. Mother lets go of my hand. "You needn't be scared of them, Juno. Now go and dry your hair."

I hurry into the bathroom upstairs. Taking a fresh towel, I rub the ends of my hair. Somehow I feel grateful to this strange bug. It stopped me getting punished. What would have happened if Mother found out I'm practicing how to swim in the lake doesn't bear thinking about. Bracing my hands on the sink, I look in the mirror. The girl gazing back with exhaustion doesn't look like me at all anymore. She's changed. I cock my head and examine the young woman on the other side. A lot hasn't changed—her long, smooth hair, the narrow, turned-up nose, the mole on her cheek that still looks like a little heart, her dark-green eyes. Unlike her lips, which are now fuller than mine, the longer neck, and the larger breasts.

The unfamiliar person looks prettier than I feel.

I throw the wet towel into the basket and leave the bathroom. On the landing I stop outside Father's bedroom door. Maybe I should go and look after him; he hasn't come out since he got back. Mother is bringing his food up to his room. And yesterday, when I put the bunch of wildflowers on his bedside table, he was muttering in his sleep and tossing and turning restlessly. I put an ear to the door and listen. The wooden floor creaks. Father's awake. I knock cautiously.

"Yes?"

"Can I come in, Father?"

"One sec."

I hear a drawer being pushed shut and then hobbled steps. The key turns twice in the lock and Father opens the door. He's wearing padded slippers, striped pajama bottoms and nothing on top. Several layers of bandage are wrapped around his tummy.

"It's nice of you to come and see me," Father says feebly, beckoning me inside. "Come in, Juno." I enter the room, which is warm, sticky, and smells of greasy sheets.

"Shall I open the window for you?"

"No, the bloody mosquitoes will eat me alive."

I close the door behind me. Father hobbles over to a chair and pushes it to the bed. "Sit down." Then he slumps onto the mattress and awkwardly pulls the duvet over his chest. I follow him and sit beside the bed. My wildflowers on the bedside table are still in bloom.

"What happened to your glasses?" I say, looking at the chunky frames resting on his nose. The lenses are as thick as the bottom of bottles.

"I lost them in the woods," Father says, adjusting the frames on his face. "This is my replacement pair."

"They make you look older," I laugh. "Like a grandad."

"The main thing is that I can see how pretty you've become, my girl."

I'm at once reminded of the story of Little Red Riding Hood. I smirk. This is what the bearded grandmother must have looked like. All that's missing is the white bonnet.

"Listen, Juno," Father says, taking my hand. "It was a big mistake, Uncle Ole finding out about you. The situation is really serious. Nobody must see you."

"I'm sorry, Father."

"I know that, of course," he says, looking kindly at me. "And I also realize you're growing up and wanting to ask questions. About Northland and Southland." He forces a smile. "I knew the time would come when we'd have to explain everything. I'd just hoped that the moment wouldn't arrive quite so soon." Father leans over to me. "You've gotten so big, Juno. Unlike your brother, who still believes the story about the strangers."

A shiver runs down my spine. Did I hear him right? Nervously I lean forward. "Are you saying that the strangers on the other side don't exist?"

"Oh yes, they do," Father replies. "But they're not strangers."

I don't understand.

"Juno, it's time to tell you the truth. About the strangers. I sense you're beginning to question things. Understandably so. That's typical at your age. I was like that as a boy, too." Father grins, then turns serious. "It was more than twelve years ago. In Italy."

"Is that Southland?"

"Yes," Father says, adjusting his glasses. "Riccione. I...I used to work at a bank there. I was in management, responsible for all the property purchases. That means I used to sell houses and land."

My heart is beating faster. This is the first time Father has spoken candidly about the past. I suddenly feel more grown up. He trusts me.

"All over Italy." Father pauses. "I sold them for the bank. But my clients were very dangerous people, Juno. Big Italian families wanting to launder their money with me."

"What does that mean?"

"Not literally. They'd done bad things, which had earned the men lots of money. To cover their tracks, they came to me to buy apartments and houses."

"You helped the strangers?" I ask, even though I can't imagine that's true.

"In the beginning, yes." Father lets his head sink back into the pillow. "I'm not proud of what I did, Juno. But one day, during Sunday mass in Rimini, God spoke to me. He appealed to my conscience. After that I couldn't look myself in the mirror anymore. So I went to the Italian police the next day. They're the guards, you see? I testified as a state witness. I informed on the criminals and their families. In front of the tribunal, in front of the judges in Rimini."

"What happened after that?"

"They swore revenge, promising to kill all of my children in retaliation. You and Boy. That's why we were brought here to Scandinavia. To Sweden, deep in the woods, on this island. We're living on a witness protection scheme, Juno. That's why we told you to hide when Uncle Ole came. So he didn't recognize you and betray our family to the Italians."

"Northland is Sweden," I say softly, thinking of the countries on the Risk board.

"But somehow the strangers, these Italian criminals, found us. I've no idea how that could have happened." Father lays his hand on his bandaged tummy. "Mother was all for keeping my injury a secret, because she didn't want to scare you. She doesn't like you children knowing the truth. But for me it's important you understand the danger we're in at the moment."

"How many strangers are there?" I ask, and I can't help thinking of the blood in the boat and on Father's shirt.

"Five. I wounded one of them."

"And guards?"

"The police aren't going to come, Juno."

"Why not?"

Father strokes my head. "The less you know, the safer it is for all of us. For our family. To notify the guards, I'd have to row to the other side of the lake. But I'm still too weak. We have to hide here and pray the Italians don't find us before I'm better again. At some point the danger will pass. I've taken precautions. There will be other opportunities. Anyway, I've got a rifle and enough ammunition. Don't worry, my girl."

But we can't wait that long, I think.

I knock on Boy's door. He opens at once and lets me in. A handful of colored pencils are on his desk, scattered all over a large piece of paper. I must have interrupted my brother drawing. I go closer up to his picture, which shows our family in front of the red log cabin. Two grown-ups, two children, a wooden cross.

"We have to call the guards," I say moving to the open window, where I look out across the lake. "That was blood on Father's shirt."

"Of course it was."

"Did you really believe it?"

"I saw Father," Boy says, coming to stand beside me. He points at the jetty and the boat chained up there. "That night when he came back. His body was soaked in blood. Father was seriously injured, Juno. What did you think?"

I don't reply. When I think of the red paint pot in the tool shed, I suddenly feel ridiculous. Boy looks at me expectantly. I'm ashamed that I didn't trust my parents. They're doing all they can to protect us.

I hurriedly change the subject. "Listen, could I borrow your nature book for a bit?"

"Why?"

"I'm looking for a particular insect."

Boy goes over to the shelf and pulls out a very thick reference book. He leafs through the pages. "What did it look like?"

"Pine chafer," I say.

Boy checks the index, opens the book at a page near the back and says, "*Polyphylla fullo* is a type of beetle from the chafer family. Otherwise known as pine chafer. It is mostly to be found in central and southern Europe, but is rare everywhere. Its northernmost habitat is southern Sweden, its easternmost is the Balkans and the Caucasus."

"Show me," I say. Boy hands me the book.

"What's wrong?"

The chafer's body is blackish-brown with striking white speckles. Mother was wrong. It wasn't this insect that attacked me down by the lake. It was much bigger.

"Oh, nothing." I close the book again.

7

It's Friday morning. I've been woken by a noise, and I can't get back to sleep. I turn to face the alarm clock: just after four o'clock. I forgot to black out the window. Feeling hot, I push the duvet to one side. It's stuffy. I stagger to the window, squinting as I pick the little metal hook out of the latch, and push the window open. A lovely fresh breeze immediately floods my room, and with every breath of air I feel more awake. That and the vibrant dawn chorus means there's no way I'm going to get back to sleep again.

I put on my slippers and go onto the landing. The bathroom is at the far end. All is quiet in the house. I flush, wash my hands and face, hang the towel back up, and creep down into the kitchen to get a glass of milk.

Opening the fridge I put the bottle on the kitchen table. I briefly consider lighting the cooker, but I don't want to make any noise and so opt for cold milk; it'll still help me get back to sleep. Just as I'm reaching for a glass from the shelf, I hear it again: the noise that woke me. I whip around to the window. A cracking, like someone breaking dry branches. Moving over to the back door that leads into the garden, I stare through the window.

A magpie hops inquisitively through our vegetable patch. I see glittering birch leaves in the wind. My eyes roam to the left. A second magpie, on the rim of the stone well. It flaps to the ground and prances around my sister's grave. In the shade of the spruces, all I can see are its white feathers moving through the thick grass in short skips. But what was that, in the distance? I screw up my eyes. Did I just see the dark figure of a bear by the shore?

I've never seen a bear in real life before, only the ones in Boy's scholarly nature books, so I can't really tell. Father told us that animals live in the woods on the other side. Is it possible that one has swum over to our island? I press my nose against the window. The glass mists up, obscuring my view. I wipe the condensation away with the sleeve of my nightie. Can bears swim? I've no idea. But the figure I saw was at least as tall as a man.

I open the back door and go out into the garden. The distant hoot of an owl echoes up from the lake. The air is mild, a gentle breeze is blowing. Wrapping my arms around my body, I duck as I go down the narrow sandy path, past the vegetable patch and our old tool shed. With each step, sharp stones dig into my thin felt soles. I grit my teeth. Only a few more paces until the small patch of grass, then I'm at the well and leap to take cover. After a deep breath, I listen carefully in the dim light of daybreak.

All I can hear are the usual rustling of the birch trees and the chorus of crickets chattering in the meadow. I was always the best when we played our games of hide-and-seek in the summer. If there's one thing I'm especially good at, it's sneaking up on people silently and unnoticed. I've used this talent of mine to scare Father to death on several occasions. That's why I'm not at all afraid now. I know every square meter of this island like the back of my hand; nature is my home. Cautiously I peek above the well. The unfamiliar shape is nowhere to be seen. But I know the direction the bear must have gone. He headed for the lake, exactly where I was attacked by the gigantic black beetle this morning.

One last glance back at our cabin to check it's all quiet, then I creep from bush to tree through the wet, waist-high reeds, past my sister's grave until eventually I find a new hiding place behind an old spruce. I look down: ugh! My nightie is sticking to my thighs like a second skin. I pull the damp material away from my legs.

Then I hear a squelch. From the reeds in front of me. I freeze like a deer when it senses danger. Curious, I put my head to one side and try to work out what the strange sloshing is. It sounds like something large is stalking through the muddy marshland, hunting for food. The bear, I think. It must have swum to our island. Boy's never going to believe me when I tell him.

Supporting myself on the trunk, I peep out from behind the spruce. A fine veil of mist shrouds the lake. My gaze drifts across the knee-high grasses, individual rocks, moss-covered branches, and brittle root wood. And then I see him amongst the reeds.

Not a bear.

It's a boy—on our island! Prowling through the reeds as elegantly as a panther, pushing the grasses aside with flowing motions. I look more intently. He's at least five years older than me, wearing a black jumper with a hood sewn onto it, dark-gray trousers, black lace-up shoes, and a black backpack on his back. He's searching the ground with a small light in his hand. The boy looks focused. The color of his face is darker than mine, and his straggly black hair falls over his forehead. From this distance I can't make out the color of his eyes, but they're definitely dark, brown perhaps, and his delicate face is graced with a slim nose. Suddenly he stops, lowers his head and stares down at his feet. The boy stranger looks around nervously, before bending down deep amongst the reeds and picking up something spider-like from the ground.

The black insect! The creature isn't moving. I must have killed it with my towel; its bent legs are sticking out stiffly from its body.

The boy presses the beetle's legs together, opens the zip of his rucksack and puts the dead, rigid creature into it. Is he an insect researcher, perhaps? That would at least provide a logical explanation, because this beetle seems to be a really rare variety that isn't even in Mother's nature book. As I lean further forward to see if he's got a butterfly net, I lose my balance.

I stumble over a tree root and am just able to break my fall with my hands. Mud squirts everywhere—onto my nightie, my face. For a moment I stay in this position as silently as possible, breathing shallowly through my mouth and looking around. I'm up to my arms in the mud; grass is tickling my nose and cheeks. I can hear a movement in the reeds. Footsteps coming closer, in my direction.

A pair of black shoes appears before my eyes. Alarmed, I look up. A helping hand is stretched out toward me. After a brief hesitation, I take hold of it. The boy carefully helps me up. I clutch his forearm with both hands and feel the muscles beneath his black jumper. They're as firm as mooring ropes.

When I'm on my feet again I let go of his arm. Out of the corner of his eye, he shyly watches me adjust my nightie. He offers me his hand.

At once I feel terrified. My heart is hammering against my chest. Is he a…? A stranger? A vengeful being from the other shore?

I swallow; my throat is dry. Is he going to kill me? Have they found us? Our hiding place, our island?

The boy stranger gives me a smile that is curiously intimate. I don't move. I can't. I can't move a muscle. If I'd only known what a stranger looks like, an *Italian*.

Impossible, I think. Pull yourself together, Juno, he can't be a stranger. Think about it, look! He doesn't seem dangerous at all. On the contrary, look at his eyes! Sparkling like the moonlight on the dark-brown water. Friendly and open. The soft features of his face, the tender smile on his lips. Who is he? My thoughts are going around and around like a hungry osprey trying to catch its prey. Maybe he's a guard come to protect us?

His large, dark-brown eyes look me up and down, and he still hasn't said a word. I'm embarrassed that he's seeing me like this—half naked and filthy—and I wrap my arms around my chest.

"*Scusa*, may I?" he asks. He has a strange accent, and his finger wipes away a small clump of mud from my cheek. A jolt shoots through my body.

"Who are you?" I say, quivering. "A guard?"

Instead of an answer, he puts the heavy backpack on the marshy ground, takes off his jumper and hands it to me. I shake my head. "What are you doing here?"

The boy stranger looks at me in silence. Then he turns to the shore in search of help. I sense he feels as uncomfortable in this situation as I do. He nervously shifts his weight from one foot to another. I breathe a sigh of relief. He can't be an *Italian*, I think, or I'd have been dead by now.

"Are you a beetle collector?" I ask, to break the odd silence, pointing at his backpack.

"*Come hai detto?*" he whispers, following my finger. Then he looks me in the eye again and shakes his head. "*Ragazza*, you should never have seen me."

"What are you doing on our island?"

"I just came to get something back," he says softly. "*Il capo* sent me."

"I see. And what have you come to get?"

He doesn't reply. I try again: "What's your name?"

The boy hesitates, biting his lower lip. It strikes me that his lips are really beautiful. Bravely, I take a step toward him. I've never stood this close to someone I don't know. Apart from Uncle Ole, of course, but he's an old man with wrinkled skin and greasy hair.

"Luca," he replies. Nice name, I think: short and yet so soft. It matches his mysterious appearance, his handsome nose and unkempt black hair. And those eyes. The corners of my mouth twitch upward involuntarily. Even though I ought to be afraid, wary.

"Juno," I say, placing my hand on my chest for clarification. I can feel my heart hopping all over my body. "My name is Juno."

"The Roman goddess," the boy preempts me as he puts his backpack over his shoulder. "Saturn's beautiful daughter." He smiles again. Luca has shining white teeth. "But that's not your real name, is it?"

I don't understand.

"*Va bene*," Luca says, cocking his head. I can see a small scar on his neck. "You speak excellent German. Better than I ever learned how to." Then he frowns. "What is your surname?"

I take a step back again. Why's the boy asking me so many questions all of a sudden? Surely it's me who ought to be getting a few answers. I mean, *he's* the one who turned up illegally on our island in the middle of the night.

Luca seems to sense my uncertainty. "I'm sorry, Juno. I didn't mean to frighten you." He tentatively holds out his hand. "But *il capo*..." He wavers and turns back to the shore. A duck flies across the water, quacking.

"What is that strange creature you put in your backpack?" My question sounds harsher than intended. "The beetle?"

Luca bows his head rather than answer. He runs his hand through his tousled hair, seemingly searching for an explanation. Those locks shine as black as the lucky stone on my bedside table. Maybe it's a sign from God that I'm drawn to thinking about my stone at this moment. I look at Luca. No, no way. He can't be a stranger. There's not a fiber in his body that looks menacing. On the contrary, he looks rather...cute.

But the answer to my question seems to weigh heavily on his shoulders. I know this feeling. When Mother asks me things I can only answer with a lie. In a weirdly familiar way, I suddenly recognize myself in him and regret the embarrassment I've caused. He seems to be very scared of his *capo*. Maybe that's his strict father, I think. Luca raises his head and looks me in the eye for a long while. "You've gotten big, Juno. Not a kid anymore, but a young lady."

I feel a strange tingling all over my body. *A young lady*. I'm lost for words. I don't know what to do. Luca is rocking from side to side, waiting for a reaction. The blood is rising to my cheeks. We just stand there, not saying anything. I've never heard the crickets chirp more loudly. A wild, frenzied chorus in my ears.

"I've got to go back now, before they notice," he then says, checking his watch. "It was nice meeting you," he says, taking a couple of paces toward me. A sweet fragrance of almonds and citrus fruits sails into my nose.

A gentle shudder runs down my spine and all the way to my toes.

Luca looks at me nervously. "But this has to remain a secret, Juno. You mustn't tell anyone that you found me on your island. It's absolutely secret, *hai capito?* This never happened!" It sounds like he's begging me. "Promise!"

I nod. Even though I don't really understand why I can't tell anyone. Boy would turn green with envy if he knew that I'd met someone from the other side of the lake. But maybe it is in fact better to keep quiet. How would Mother react? Or Father? I can't bear the thought of Father wading through the reeds with his rifle to shoot Luca. Just because he thinks the boy stranger is one of those so-called *Italians*.

But Luca is a guard. He can't be anything else. No question. I can sense it. I just *know*. It's hard to describe in words. This strange tempest of feelings inside my body. It struck me like lightning.

Unexpectedly.

And bizarrely. In his presence I feel secure, understood, and protected. Unlike with Mother. Even though we only met a few minutes ago. Is that crazy?

No, Luca isn't a stranger. Never.

But what is it, this exhilarating fluttering in my tummy? It's a new feeling for me. And it's good. Does he feel the same?

Luca also said I've gotten big, didn't he? Which means he must have been watching me for some time. Probably with binoculars from the other side of the lake.

Luca is a guard.

He's watching over me.

"*Bene*," he says, turning around and jogging down to the water. I follow each one of his steps until he stops a few meters from the shore and unties a thin rope. Now I can see his black dinghy, too. It's hidden in the tall reeds. He tosses his backpack and jumper in, leaps onto the seat, and reaches for the paddles.

"Will you come back?" I call after him. The words just slip out. Rashly, but from deep inside my heart. Luca turns around in surprise, stares at me for a while, then lowers his head. The hood reveals more of his face. An eternity goes by. There's a stabbing pain in my tummy; I feel sick. And an indescribable fear that I'll never see him again. What if he says no?

"Saturday night, 2:00 a.m.? Here by the shore?" Luca calls.

I could embrace the whole of Northland.

8

Mother takes my soup bowl and tips the vegetable broth back into the pot. I haven't touched it. Just as I didn't touch breakfast, lunch, and yesterday's supper, which Mother cut into small pieces for me. In heart shapes, like when I was a little girl and in bed with a temperature. But her efforts were in vain; I haven't been hungry since Friday. I'm certain even the tiniest morsel would make me sick.

"I'm going down to the lake!" Boy says, leaping up from the table and taking his plate to the sink. "Are you coming, Juno?"

Mother stands next to me. "I'm not sure that's a good idea." She lays her hand on my forehead; her fingers are as cold as ice. "Your sister ought to rest some more. She wasn't in bed all day yesterday for no reason."

"I'm not sick, Mother," I say. But to be honest, I'm not so sure. I've never felt as weird as this. It's like trolls are doing somersaults in my belly. If only it were night already and I could see Luca again, I think, getting up from my chair.

Mother puts an arm around me and strokes a hair from my face.

"I know it's all very unsettling. But don't worry, children, the strangers will never find us here. Our island is well hidden." Then she takes her arm away, goes to the sink and turns on the tap. "And Father will be better again soon."

"If they haven't found us yet, Juno, then they haven't got a clue where we live," Boy says, nodding confidently. It's unlike him to try and comfort me. But I expect he's saying it more to himself.

"That's our hope, too," Mother concurs, as she soaks the bowls with a bar of soap. "Don't you worry. We'll always be watching over you."

I put my unused water glass back in the kitchen cupboard and follow my brother into the garden.

We sit on the big rock, throwing stones into the lake. I'm glad we're silent, because I'm not up for chatting. I can't begin to describe how I feel; I don't know what's happening to me. It's like my head is stuffed with cotton wool. I'm listless and tired, but also excited. Luca is on my mind all the time; I can't help it. My plan to leave the island is disappearing ever further into a fog of inner turmoil. I could uproot trees or crawl beneath my duvet. This restlessness is driving me mad. And nobody can help me.

I feel lonely.

"Do you think about her much?"

"What?" I turn to Boy, confused.

"Our sister," he says, reaching for a stone the size of his hand and hurling it into the water.

"Not much anymore," I reply, watching the ripples on the surface of the water. "It was such a long time ago."

"Was she nice?"

I don't answer. Why does he want to talk about this now? Haven't we got enough on our plate at the moment? I sink my head, wishing I were invisible. But it doesn't help; Boy taps me on the shoulder.

"What?"

"Tell me about her." Boy's beginning to annoy me.

"She had short, black hair," I say. "And she was like a beanpole."

"The opposite of you, then." Boy laughs. "What else?"

"Her skin was as white as milk."

My brother narrows his eyes. "Before Father pulled her out of the water or afterward?"

"Even before," I say, hoping that this conversation will soon come to an end. "Look, Boy, I was only five years old when it happened." Suddenly I see it all in my mind again. The gray storm clouds in the sky, Mother on her knees, screaming, on the damp ground, her hands covering her eyes, and Father laying the blue-checkered woolen blanket on top of the lifeless body, a single shoe by the shore. "I've only got a dim memory of it all."

"Was she really trying to swim to the other side?"

I think of the lucky stone she gave me, shiny and black, the evening before the accident. *This stone will protect you always*, my big sister said. *It's very special, Juno*. I shudder.

Because it's from the other side.

9

I sit on the tree stump in my nightie and wait. It slowly gets light. The lake lies silently before me; the only sounds to be heard are the throaty chirping of the crickets in the tall reeds and the eerie cooing and clicking of a capercaillie.

I'd set the alarm for midnight, then tossed and turned sleeplessly in bed, one eye always on the clock. The time just wouldn't pass. To take my mind off things, I'd leafed through my book of Hans Christian Andersen tales, but I was too distracted to take in the *Thumbelina* story. Even though I know by heart the tale of the lonely girl who falls in love with a tiny fairy prince with wings. Then, finally, at a quarter to two, I jumped out of bed, put on my red sandals and cardigan, and slipped out the kitchen door.

Now I'm holding the black stone. It's smooth and cold. My eyes wander to the other side of the lake. But I can't see anything.

No movement, no boat, no Luca.

I clench my fist, squeeze the lucky stone, and make a wish for Luca to appear soon so I can question him about Northland and Southland.

Maybe Luca can even tell me if he's seen the strangers in the village on the other side, the so-called *Italians* Father strongly warned me about. And if there are lots of lucky stones like this over there.

Opening my hand, I gaze at the shiny stone that looks like a black pearl in the palm of my hand.

My big sister actually managed to swim across the lake undetected. She'd just turned nine. But why did she come back? I would have definitely stayed over there to discover the big wide world.

I close my eyes and picture her wandering in the moonlight through the dense undergrowth, searching the shore on the other side for shiny lucky stones. Her white, floor-length nightie hovers above the dark-green moss and rusty-brown leaves, and it brushes the branch of a birch tree. Beside her trots a deer that timidly raises its head, sticks its nose into the wind and smells. My sister strokes its brown coat, then the two of them head deeper into the dark spruce wood, side by side. A source of light appears above them, a mist elf with wings, guiding them to the mysterious city. Then suddenly, a plop on the surface of the water, followed by continuous gentle splashing. The deer freezes, pricks up its ears, and its large dark eyes stare back at me on the island.

The call of a tawny owl tears me from my thoughts.

I look up.

Just a few meters away, an adder is winding its way across the pitch-black surface of the water, in search of an unsuspecting victim. Staying perfectly still I watch the small waves it draws in its wake until the adder soon disappears from view into the thick reeds. I offer my hope to the little voles in their lair that they survive the morning, then focus again on the other side of the lake. And I wait. I wait longingly in my hiding place.

I don't know how much time has passed, but it's getting lighter and the birds louder. I can't see a boat anywhere. Still no Luca. Did he get the wrong day? Or did I? Today is Saturday, isn't it? Two in the morning. Actually…it's Sunday morning. Oh no, was he here last night, waiting in vain for me?

Since Friday I've lost all sense of time. Minutes pass like hours, hours like days. Nervously, I jiggle the lucky stone in my hand. No, Luca said Saturday night, I'm absolutely certain. And that's today. So, why's he not here?

Maybe something happened to him on the way? And now he's lying injured in the woods? All alone and helpless. No sooner has this unmentionable thought crossed my mind than my arms and legs start to cramp. My upper body is as stiff as the loudspeaker mast for our sirens. The strangers!

Yes, maybe the strangers killed him.

I squeeze the stone in my hand until my fingers hurt. Calm down, Juno, he's bound to be alive. Your mind's just playing tricks on you. Too many thoughts, too many *maybes*. You can't think clearly. There are many logical reasons why he might not be here.

Luca is a guard; he'll turn up soon.

He won't, the voice suddenly whispers in my head. As softly as the lighting of a matchhead. Small and insignificant. But soon the dry straw catches fire, spreading unchecked across my soul and I realize the true reason why Luca's not here. It's so simple. Because I was unwilling to admit it to myself and I'm still looking for excuses.

It's because of me. Of course. I'm the reason. He didn't have the courage to tell me he doesn't like me. *Pretty?* Forget it. He was just trying to be friendly. Didn't want to hurt me when I begged to see him again.

I'm so stupid. How could I think that he likes me, too? I begin to despair. Of me, of this secret meeting.

Suddenly I feel cold. My nightie sticks clammily to my skin. One last time I desperately scan the opposite shore. No, Juno, he's not going to come. Not today, and not tomorrow either. Never.

Furious, I hurl my lucky stone into the reeds and stomp back to the house.

10

I turn to my alarm clock, blinking. It's Sunday, just after half past two. The afternoon sun is shining on the abundant breakfast tray that lies untouched on my bedside table. Mother must have put it there while I was asleep. I didn't get a wink of sleep during the night. I can't remember when I finally nodded off, but I do recall the dream I had soon afterward.

I dreamed I was skipping through an endless, honey-scented field of flowers, past wild roses, twinflowers, fire lilies, and cornflowers, when from nowhere a dark-brown water hole opened up in front of me. I stopped and stared at the stinky puddle in the middle of all these flowers. Two newly hatched ducklings were swimming on it, their feathers dark and sticky. They were beating their wings, cheeping and in danger of drowning at any minute. As I bent down to save them, I stumbled over a tree root and fell headfirst into the sludgy water. The foul quagmire enveloped me at once and pulled me down ever deeper into the blackness as if I were tied to a rope. I flailed my arms and legs wildly until the water suddenly became clear and pure. I could see again, breathe again. All around me were colorful fish, dancing mermaids, and aquatic plants glowing green. A young prince with a golden crown swam toward me with powerful strokes. It was Luca. He smiled as he held out his hand. I was about to take it when it turned into black ink, dissolving into nothingness, and I woke up.

Unnerved, I push the duvet to the side and turn to face the window. The curtains are open. A crane glides past in the blue, cloudless sky. Why didn't Luca come? Why doesn't he like me anymore? Does he think I'm too ugly? I want to die on the spot. Simply stop breathing because of the heartache.

I bury my head beneath the sweaty pillow, hiding from my own shame, when there's a knock at my door.

"Juno?" It's Boy. "Everything OK?"

Go away, I shout in my thoughts, leave me alone forever! But he knocks again. When I don't answer, the door opens a crack. Hesitant steps. They come closer, fall silent by my bed, then the pillow is yanked away.

"It's Sunday. Games day. Don't you want to play?"

The heavenly aroma of blueberry cake drifts through the door.

"I'm sick," I grunt.

"No, you're not," Boy says, touching my forehead. "You're not at all hot."

I shake his hand away.

"Mother's baked a cake. And our Sunday isn't fun without you. Even Father's coming down to join in. And I'll let you decide what we play."

"Don't want to," I say, turning away from him in defiance. But Boy doesn't seem to be interested in my feelings. He saunters around the bed, whistling, and flops down onto the mattress.

"Anything apart from Risk," he grins, reaching without asking for the full glass of elderflower lemonade on my breakfast tray, and emptying it in a single gulp. Annoyed, I take a deep breath. My nostrils are filled with fruity berries and warm caramel. It smells delicious.

"You owe me one anyway, Juno," he says, putting the glass back. In the very place where my black lucky stone was yesterday. "After last week when you ruined our games afternoon with your questions about Northland and Southland."

My beloved lucky stone. Why did I toss it into the reeds? It's not the stone's fault that Luca didn't turn up at our agreed meeting point.

"Come on; the game will take your mind off things," Boy says. "Like that time at supper when you got such a fright, remember? Because there was blood running down your leg..." He points at my legs under the duvet.

"For God's sake, shut up!" I shout, pulling the duvet off and jumping out of bed, embarrassed. My very first period. "That's none of your business!"

Boy looks decidedly confused. "It didn't happen again, did it?" he says, putting his head to one side. He looks at me in horror. "Did you hurt your leg again?"

"No," I hiss, hurrying to the wardrobe—I have to end this conversation now. Out of the corner of my eye, I can see him follow me with his gaze. "Alright, alright, let's play a game!" I snap over my shoulder, pulling my striped summer dress from the hanger. "Wait for me downstairs."

Mother points to the yellow-spotted vase on the dining table. Boy shakes his head vigorously. She spins around to the shelves and pauses for a moment. "The encyclopedia, top row, far left?" My brother says no again. Pursing her lips, Mother turns back to us at the table, strokes the crocheted tablecloth pensively and says, "What about the milk jug?"

"Not that, either!" Boy drums the top of the table with his palms. "You've had ten guesses, Mother. You lost!"

"What was it, then?"

"The yellow button on your blouse!" Boy laughs. "You didn't think of that!" Mother looks down, surprised, then joins in the laughter. I don't know what's so funny about it. I lick the cream off the spoon and put it back on the plate. The sweetened whipped cream lifts my mood—a little bit, at least. I could scrape the entire bowl clean.

"To finish, it's your turn again, Juno," Father says, putting another forkful of cake in his mouth.

"If I have to," I say, looking around the living room. My eyes skim the embroidered cushions on the green sofa, the framed painting of water lilies on the wall, the row of plants on the windowsill, the golden wall clock, the woven wicker chair, the white china owls on the mantelpiece, and then back to Boy again.

"I spy with my little eye..." Here I'd love to say *a stranger*, because this pretend cheerfulness is getting on my nerves. Didn't Father say we were in danger? I don't see anything that looks like danger here. Happy faces with coffee, cocoa, and cake. As if nothing had ever happened. But I don't want to ruin Boy's sacred games afternoon again, so I say, "Something black."

Boy immediately begins guessing. He lists all the things he can see from his chair: Father's black binoculars, the charcoal in the fire, the record player, and a few other things. I don't really listen to him; I just keep shaking my head.

"Wrong," I say tersely when he's named the tenth black object. "You lost."

But I knew that before we started. Boy will never guess the answer. How could he? I mean, he doesn't know Luca. Let alone his heart.

"Let me have one more guess, OK?" Boy pleads. "I'll definitely work out what it is."

"To find something you have to know what you're looking for," I counter, breaking up a crumb of cake on my plate with my fingernail.

"Give me a second chance!" he says. "Please, Juno!"

Mother gives me a harsh look. Father turns to me, too, and the expression on his face says that, as the elder sister, I should indulge him. Play happy families.

"Alright," I say, crossing my arms in front of my chest. "You've got one final guess." Boy thanks me profusely and scans the room as if he were trying to solve a difficult sum. He takes his time with his answer, then points tentatively at the window behind me. I turn around and look down at the lake.

"Correct!" I say, even though I've no idea what he's seen down there. I don't care, either. Right now all I can think of is his plea: *Give me a second chance!*

I'm chewing over these words. Why should I give my brother a second chance but not Luca? Even though Luca didn't ask for one. How could he? I mean, it's possible there's a simple reason why he couldn't come. And he does like me. He said I was *pretty*. I don't know who to believe anymore.

Boy springs from his chair in delight. "I was right, wasn't I Juno? I said I'd work it out. You've got no secrets from me!"

"What was it, then?" Mother asks, surprised, and Father looks at me expectantly, too. I open my mouth and hesitate. Shit, what am I going to say? Quick, I've got to find some object—

"There! On the window!" Boy exclaims, running around the table to the large sitting-room window and tapping on the two black bird stickers on the glass.

"Well done, Boy!" Father says, getting out of his chair. "Right, that's enough of I spy. I need to lie down again. I think that was quite enough excitement for me. My wound is starting to hurt again."

Mother and I clear the table, then I go to my room, too. I drop onto the bed with my arms outstretched and forge a plan. For tonight.

I'm going to give us a second chance.

11

The sun had only set a few hours before the alarm clock finally went off. A quarter to two in the morning. I'd lain awake in bed and carefully folded my slip over the clock's metal bells to avoid waking anyone. After quickly putting on my scratchy cardigan, I ran down the creaking stairs and slipped out into the garden via the kitchen door. It was mild with a gentle breeze wafting through the birch leaves.

Now I'm here, at our meeting point, one day later. I wade through the head-high reeds, looking for my lucky stone. If I'm lucky I'll find that, at least. Around me the crickets are singing their early morning song as I shuffle through the boggy ground. Damp air settles on my cheeks. I know exactly where I tossed the stone. But it's as black as the ground I'm trudging across. I hope I don't wake any adders as I'm scouring the wild grasses. Carefully I push every single stalk aside. Nothing but mud and startled grasshoppers who leap away in all directions like raindrops. I'm just about to turn around to search further to the left when I spot the black shiny surface. It's staring at me a few centimeters away from the furrowed mud. I reach my fingers into the sludge and pluck it out. My lucky stone! Brimming with joy, I march down to the shore and clean it in the water. How incredible to have found it amongst all those other stones. Now I know it's a lucky stone for sure. Rubbing it dry on my jumper, I press it to my heart.

As I look up, just a few meters away a rubber dinghy emerges from the morning mist. I hold my breath. Luca! He's come! He rows energetically to the shore. I jump up and down. Thank you, my lucky stone. Thank you for this second chance.

The oars pull through the dark water one last time, then Luca springs out of the boat and ties it to a tree root. His head bowed, he shuffles over to me, his hood pulled down over his eyes. I search his face for a smile, but there's nothing. No expectant chuckle, no cheeky grin. Isn't he pleased to see me? I take two steps back. Luca lifts his head.

We look at each other.

Everything's bubbling up inside me, so many questions. I fidget impatiently. Why's he not saying anything? Is he ashamed because he didn't turn up yesterday? He pushes the hood off his head. His eyes look curiously empty and exhausted.

"Where were you?" The words come blurting out.

He merely points at a fallen tree trunk in the reeds. I don't move a muscle. Luca sits on the trunk and opens the zip of his hooded jumper.

"I'm really sorry, Juno," he says eventually, pulling his arms out of the sleeves. He spreads out the black material over the damp bark and pats it. "Come and sit down here, please."

I pull myself together and sit on his jumper, anticipating an explanation. But Luca just stares over at the other side of the lake.

For several minutes we sit there in silence. There's no way I'm going to be the one to start. I mean, I was the one who came here yesterday like we'd agreed. I don't need to explain myself. Luca turns to me. "I can't stay long, Juno."

"Why didn't you come?"

"I couldn't," he says softly. "My *capo* had important things to discuss with us. Heated discussions that went on late into the night."

"I waited at an hour for you at least."

"It's more complicated than you think, Juno."

"I was worried about you."

"Do you think I was any different?" Luca rubs his face with both hands. "I thought about you all night and didn't get a wink of sleep."

My heart dances with joy. He *does* like me, then. I squeeze the lucky stone in my hand.

"Juno, it's really very dangerous for me to come and see you on the island," he says, giving me a long stare. "For you, too."

"I don't care."

"Listen. They don't know I'm with you." Luca looks at his watch. "And they must never find out. *Posso contare su di te?*"

"Who? The strangers?"

Luca's thoughts seem to be elsewhere. In a very dark place. "I only came to make sure they hadn't done anything bad to you."

"I'm fine," I say in quick response to reassure him. But that's a lie. I've been almost sick with heartache. Was it heartache? It's a new feeling for me, hard to describe. Like hot and cold at the same time, loud and soft, wild, and gentle. "I've missed you terribly."

He looks at me with large eyes.

"They must never find out that I've gone away illicitly, Juno. Come over to the island again to see you." Luca is jiggling his leg nervously. "I'm sorry, I've got to leave again now. Otherwise I'll jeopardize their plan. And then I'll be badly punished. And you..." he says, hesitating, "you could end up dead."

Dead?

"But I won't let that happen. Never," he says, placing a hand on my shoulder. It's warm and soft. "I'm going to protect you, Juno. I'll come back tomorrow night, and then I'll explain everything. I promise."

12

It's cold and rainy. Quite fitting for this sad Monday afternoon. It should be Uncle Ole day, but the old postman didn't come. Mother is convinced he's fallen ill. Not surprising in this weather. Father spent the whole morning waiting impatiently by our front door. Ready at any moment to give us children the order to hide. I could see that the waiting made him angry. Eventually he gave up and went back to his sickbed. This is the first time I've been able to understand Father's anger.

Impatience is an insect bite you mustn't scratch.

Uncle Ole just didn't turn up. But I didn't mind, because it meant Boy and I could spend time in the vegetable garden, picking berries for our porridge. Until the summer storm turned more violent.

Lost in thought I stare out of the sitting-room window. The images from last night are still playing in my mind, as hazy as the veil of mist above our lake.

Luca hugging me.

Luca getting into his boat.

Luca disappearing into the darkness.

But I'm going to see him again tonight. He'll stay longer, he said. He's going to explain everything. The prospect of our nighttime meeting makes me feel so happy that I don't want to waste any more thoughts on Luca's warning.

You could end up dead.

"Juno?" I hear Mother's voice right beside me. "We're waiting for your answer."

I turn around and look at the nature book, which is open on the table in front of me. "Sorry, Mother. OK, the great crested grebe–"

"No cheating!" Boy interrupts me. "Without looking at the book."

"Yeah, yeah," I say, trying to remember our lesson. "The great crested grebe is an aquatic bird, active during the day. A species from the grebe family. Its Latin name is—"

Mother shuts my book. "I think we'd be better off checking your maths. That's the end of nature for today." Smiling, she pushes the exercise book and pen toward me. "OK, Juno, what's thirty-eight times four?"

"One hundred and fifty-two," I reply seconds later without having touched the pencil.

"No guessing," Boy grumbles.

"I didn't," I say. Mental arithmetic is one of my strengths. Even though I rarely let it show to avoid making my brother look bad. He finds maths hard. Like me with love. But I've only been aware of this since meeting Luca. Boy grabs my sheet of paper and checks my calculation. Mother watches him. He looks up, bewildered. "That's correct."

Mother gives a nod of satisfaction. "Three hundred and thirty divided by six."

I close my eyes and imagine myself back down by the shore. In the reeds in front of me, between the birch trees, two digits appear, glowing pink. They're human-sized and side by side as if holding hands. "Fifty-five."

"How does she do that?" I hear Boy say from far away. "Is that right, Mother?"

"Work it out."

If only everything were as simple as maths. Do one and one really make two? Only Luca can answer that question. Why can't I help thinking of him every minute? Of his eyes, his hair, his hands, and lips? Deep in my heart I feel we have a very special connection. Like a clock and a hand, a shoe and shoelace. We just belong together, Luca and me. Like the bolt in a hinge—without each other we would fall apart. But does Luca feel the same way?

"Yes," Boy says; I open my eyes. "It's the right answer."

Dawn greets me. The storm has passed. The weather has mood swings, too. I gaze longingly at the lake, at Luca's dinghy. He's just a few meters from our island, pulling through the water with both oars. I kiss my lucky stone and put it in my cardigan. Then I jump up and run toward him as he ties the boat to the tree trunk. He's wearing the same jumper as yesterday, dark-blue trousers and black boots.

"Have you been waiting long?" he asks, removing his hood.

"No," I reply with a smile; the blood in my right forefinger begins to throb.

"*Scusa*," he says, sitting wearily on a rock and wiping his face with his sleeve.

"The main thing is, you're here," I say, putting my arms behind my back. Luca gives me a nod; I sit next to him. When our arms make brief contact, my heart almost stops.

"I snuck away," Luca says, turning to me. "Nobody suspects a thing. But every night it's getting riskier, do you understand? *Il capo* has other plans. And I have disobeyed his instructions. For you, Juno. Even though I've only been on it for a few months." His tanned face is just a few centimeters from mine. "So we have to hurry."

I raise my eyebrows. "With what?"

"We're all over there in the Nääs Fabriker," Luca says, pointing across the lake. "Do you know the hotel?"

I shake my head. *Hotel?*

"The rooms are fine. Brick walls, white wood, and lots of steel—all very modern. It's an old factory. The hotel even has a heated outside pool." He looks at me, puzzled. "Have you ever been to the town over there?"

I shake my head again.

"Never been to Tollered?"

All of a sudden, I feel ashamed at having spent my entire life on the island. At not understanding what Luca's talking about. Even though he speaks my language.

I rest my chin on my chest.

His mouth is now very close to my left ear. I can sense his breath on my neck, smell his sweet almond aroma. "I was thinking about you all day long. You are in grave danger."

I feel a pleasant tingling sensation all over my body and just want to throw my arms around him.

"That's why I'm really worried about you. And that's also the reason why..." He hesitates briefly. "Why I'm risking my job tonight to save you." Luca takes a deep breath. "I can't sit around waiting in this hotel any longer. Especially now they've analyzed my drone images."

"What do you mean 'save'?" I ask. "What sort of images?"

"*Mi dispiace*," Luca says, reaching into the front pocket of his jumper and taking out a small photograph. "I shouldn't be showing you this, but..." He hands me the picture.

Confused, I look at the young, blond woman by the shore of the lake.

She's not smiling.

"The photograph was sent to my *capo* four days ago."

How is that possible? It's me, beside Uncle Ole's boat.

"That's why we're here, Juno," he whispers. Out of the corner of my eye I can see Luca turning to me, a large, black shadow, as powerful as a bear. "Can you tell me how many other people live here on the island?"

"Just Mother and Father," I reply, lost in thought, the photo still in my trembling hands. "And my little brother." I'm feverishly trying to work it all out. How can this be? Where did this picture of me come from? Uncle Ole must have taken it with his little black case. Was that a camera?

"*Fratello?*" Luca asks, sounding surprised. "You have a brother?"

"Boy," I reply. "He's twelve."

"*Oh, merda!*" His voice seems far away.

My head is spinning.

"It's old high German," I say, my thoughts still churning over the meeting with Uncle Ole and the strange black object he took from his dirty coat pocket. "Boy's name."

Even years before we arrived on the island, Mother and Father knew what they were going to call us. As Mother had always longed for children, my first name was to be a hopeful omen for her plans.

Juno, the Roman goddess of birth.

I always liked the idea that, with my name, I was responsible for our family's happiness. Unlike my little brother, whose name in Frisian simply means *the younger one*. As if Mother had suspected that Boy would be the third born.

"Does your Father have a gun?" Luca says, breaking my chain of thought. He gives me a severe look.

I'm just about to tell him that we've got a rifle in our safe room beneath the kitchen when my eyes focus once more on the photo in my hands.

If Uncle Ole really did take a picture of me illicitly, why did he send it to Luca's *capo*? Didn't I promise not to tell my parents anything?

I suddenly feel icily cold.

To get the payment, the gold that is a reward for us. The word *bounty* flashes in my mind. My entire body starts to shiver.

"I'm really very sorry, Juno." Luca puts his hand on my shoulder. I shake it off in panic and leap to my feet.

"Why are you here?" I shout.

He doesn't answer me.

I take a step toward him and shove the photo under his nose. "You're one of them, aren't you? You're a stranger! From Southland, from Italy. You want to take revenge on Father!"

Luca bows his head.

"That's why you've been watching me!" An unexpected rage surges inside me. "Is that why you came to the island? Because you mean to kill us all?"

He shakes his head.

"Why, then?" I say, my voice quivering. "You wounded Father badly! I'm so stupid! I thought you were a guard. I trusted you!"

Luca raises his head. Then, bracing his hands on his thighs, he leans forward and stands up. He is a head taller than me.

"Many years have passed since Riccione."

"What do you want from us?"

No answer. Instead he stares at me, and in his eyes, I can see him desperately searching for words. The corners of his mouth twitch. He rubs his face with both hands as if he were washing it, then looks up at the sky and takes a deep breath.

"I'd planned to get you off the island tonight by myself," Luca says softly. "But that's not going to happen anymore." He pauses. "Because you say you've got a brother."

I frown. What's he talking about? What has Boy got to do with all of this?

Luca comes toward me and offers me his hand, but I recoil. "It's not what you think, Juno." Luca stops. "You've got to understand that we had to be absolutely sure you were the girl on Blomquist's photo."

"What's that supposed to mean?" I ask.

My voice is cracking. When Luca reaches behind him, I jump back. He takes a folded piece of paper from his trouser pocket. His fingers are trembling as he opens it.

"What's that?" I say, looking in bafflement at the piece of printed paper he's holding up to my face.

It's a page from a newspaper.

I lean forward. The color photograph that takes up almost half of the thin piece of paper shows a blond, two-year-old girl on the beach.

She's sitting on a blue-and-white striped towel on the sand, holding a yellow plastic bucket. She's smiling at the camera. Moving closer to the picture I can make out a tiny baby tooth inside the mouth. Men and women are lying on the sand in the background, wearing few clothes, all with dark sunglasses.

The place seems strangely familiar.

"Your name isn't Juno," says the voice that sounds far away. "Thirteen years ago, you were abducted from Italy. You were still a little child when they kidnapped you in broad daylight. From the beach in Riccione."

I gaze at the yellow beach bucket with the funny mouse in a spotted summer dress, then my legs give way. The last thing I see through blurred eyes is Luca rushing forward to catch me.

Then everything goes black.

13

When I open my eyes, I'm in Luca's arms. He strokes a hair from my head and looks worried. I try sitting up but feel dizzy at once. Exhausted, I let my head drop again.

"I'm from Rimini, which is near Riccione," Luca says. "I'm with Interpol, working as a drone pilot with the Italian police."

"Drone?" My voice is no more than a whisper.

Luca takes a deep breath. "What you swatted with your towel wasn't an insect but a sort of flying camera. I'm sorry I made it hover so close to your head, but I needed a usable photo of your face."

I'm gradually beginning to understand why Luca turned up on the shore that night. He just wanted to recover his hissing beetle that I'd destroyed in a panic. But how can a flying camera work?

"My colleagues have been searching for you for thirteen years. People know about your abduction all over the world," Luca says hesitantly. He seems anxious to find the right words. "Especially in Rimini. Lots of people still talk about you and your kidnapping. I've only been part of the special unit for six months," he says, squeezing my hand. "But your parents have never given up hope, Elly. And Interpol and the FBI have never given up the search."

"Elly?"

"Your real name," Luca says. "Elly Watson."

"How…how can that be?" I ask feebly.

"Our informant, Ole Blomquist, must have recognized you. An old Swedish postman from Tollered. Each year we've put together a photofit picture and sent it to the newspapers. With the help of a forensic artist in England, we simulated how you might have aged over the years. And the mobile photo that Blomquist emailed to the Swedish police four days ago came up with a 92 percent match to our image."

I don't understand a word of what he's saying.

Luca looks at me. "But the heart—your mole removed any remaining doubts." He points at my cheek. "You're Elly Watson, from Cambridge, England."

Again I try to sit up; Luca carefully helps me. I'm still a bit woozy, but after a few deep breaths I feel better.

A cool wind sweeps my face.

"That's why I was surprised you speak German. I learned it at school," Luca says. Then he points in the direction of our shed. "My job was to monitor the island with a drone to find out the safest place to approach your cabin from. Without putting you in danger. Our original plan was to free you from the house as soon as the weather got better. Visibility is always bad when it's stormy. My *capo* didn't want to take any risks."

Luca falls silent and sits opposite me. His expression is one of concern. "But then something happened that made our rescue operation more urgent."

He puts his hands together as if in prayer.

"We believe your abductors know we're here in Sweden, looking for you."

"How?" I ask automatically, as if we were talking about what to have for lunch, but other questions are shooting through my mind. I dig my fingernails into my arm. Maybe this is all one bad dream I'm about to wake up from. A brief pain beneath my skin.

"Around noon today, we found a dead body," Luca says, pointing across the lake again. "Ole Blomquist. Our informant who emailed us the photo on Monday. That same day we were going to get in touch with him, but he didn't respond. My *capo* assumed he wanted to remain anonymous. But we were wrong. There was another reason. According to the Swedish coroner's office he was stabbed in the woods not long after he sent the photograph."

He takes a small, shiny black case from his trouser pocket. The device looks familiar. Luca taps the glass surface several times then swipes up with his finger. As if by magic, a photo of blood-smeared glasses appears. They're lying on the leaf-strewn ground. Right beside them is a yellow plastic sign with a number on it. "Do you recognize these?"

I stare at the silver frames.

A wild storm of images floods my head.

Full moon, white shirt. Rusty-brown water in the sink. Father's boat chained up, a black puddle. Bandages, chunky replacement glasses. The flashing puzzle pieces slowly come together in my mind.

"Father," I say softly. "They're his glasses."

Luca bites his lower lip and nods in confirmation. "That's what we thought. Blomquist didn't wear glasses."

Feeling dizzy, I use my arms to support myself on the rock. Is Luca really trying to tell me that Father killed Uncle Ole?

"You're in big danger, Elly," he whispers, placing a hand on my shoulder. It feels hot. "That's why I couldn't wait another day. I wanted to get you away from here as quickly as possible. Tonight." He breathes out and drops his head. "But I can't do that anymore, do you understand? If the people who kidnapped you realize that you're no longer on the island..." Luca falters, searching for words. "They'll take your little brother hostage. I can't run that risk."

"So what does this mean?" I ask involuntarily. I reach up to my forehead: it's clammy and cold. Behind it, hundreds of questions are buzzing like a swarm of mosquitoes. The noise is unbearable.

Luca is shifting back and forth on the rock.

"I'm really very sorry," he says. "I don't have any choice." Luca runs his fingers through his hair. "But I can't take you to the other side. Not tonight." He swallows. "Listen, you've got to go straight back to your house, before your kidnappers suspect anything." His hands are shaking. "And you mustn't let them think anything's wrong or changed. Do you understand? As far as they're concerned, you have to keep on being Juno."

No, I don't understand. I *am* Juno.

Luca takes hold of my right arm and puts the slim device into my hand. It weighs at least the same as five apples.

"This is my personal *cellulare*," he says. "You can use it to call me anytime. I'll save my work number on it."

Again he swipes his finger across the glass surface and taps the device a number of times. It makes some faint sounds. "Look here, I've put my name on the list of favorites." He points at a round picture of Luca in a dark-blue shirt. "All you have to do is tap on my photo, and then we can talk if you put the thing up to your ear. It's really simple." He gives me what I think is supposed to be a nod of encouragement. "Hide the phone in a safe place, Elly. And don't show it to anyone. As a precaution I've switched it to *Do not disturb* and disabled the passcode."

Luca checks his watch.

"I'm afraid I've got to go, now," he says, putting on his jumper and getting up. I slip the strange object into the pocket of my cardigan and get up, too.

We stand there, staring at each other in silence. I hear the hoot of an owl from the other side of the lake. And the chorus of crickets is audible once more.

Luca takes a small step toward me. I feel a faint pressure on my breastbone, above my heart. My breathing becomes slower. I sense the special connection between us again, between the stranger prince and the girl he's come to save. Like an invisible rope has been wrapped around us both.

Luca wipes his eyes with his sleeve.

And at once my veil has been wiped away, too. Reality is right before my very eyes; it's like I've just awoken from a nightmare. Only to realize that I'm still dreaming. Luca came to take me off the island tonight. Because I was abducted as a little child. From Italy. By Mother and Father.

My head is spinning again.

I feel dizzy.

"May I hug you goodbye?" he asks. I feel as if I'm going to lose my balance at any moment. I nod weakly.

Luca comes closer; I shut my eyes. He puts his arms around my shoulders. It feels good. Blood shoots to my cheeks. Luca pulls me toward him, with his subtle fragrance of citrus and sweet almond. I can feel his heart beating in his chest, his body warmth, his strong arms. Once again I have an unfamiliar sense of security, as if we'd known each other since we were born. An inner connection. There are butterflies in my tummy. Time stands still. Please, dear God, turn our bodies into marble so we never have to part.

I kiss him on the cheek.

My lips feel a jolt of electricity. Surprised, Luca opens his eyes and takes a step back. My body is shaking. A cool gust of wind blows up from the shore. I rub myself to keep warm.

"I…I'm sorry," I whisper.

"I'll write to tell you when we're coming," he says. "And please be careful, Elly." Then Luca vanishes into the reeds. I stay there for a long while, watching his rubber dinghy disappear.

Until I begin to weep silently.

PART TWO

14

On the way back I stop beside the grave of my unnamed sister and stroke the weathered wooden cross. I'm so sorry, I whisper in my head, squatting on the damp earth. I run my hand through the ankle-high grass. Who were you?

After she died, Mother and Father didn't mention her once. But over the years memories fade like paint in the frost and rain. If they're not refreshed from time to time, they disappear forever.

I pick a twinflower and lay it on her grave.

The house is quiet when I go in. I take off my shoes, creep upstairs barefoot, and collapse onto my bed in exhaustion.

Something is poking into my back. I roll to the side and take out my Hans Christian Andersen book. I was leafing through it before midnight to pass the time. It's still open at *Thumbelina*. This story has been a bit like a lucky charm for me since childhood, a real comfort, a chance to escape the island. In my imagination, at least. Could it help me now, too?

To banish my gloomy thoughts about Elly Watson.

And my desire for Luca.

The jumble inside my head.

I go back to the beginning of the story, skimming the first few lines that Mother used to read to me over and over again, once we'd finally arrived in Northland after days in the car. And during the weeks that followed, too.

My memory of back then is very hazy. Curled up in Mother's lap in front of the crackling fire, listening to the story of the little girl who was no bigger than a thumb.

I was two years old, perhaps, and couldn't understand a word of what Mother was reading to me loudly and clearly.

A woman who's desperate to have a child begs an old witch for help. She's given a magical grain of barley, which she plants in a pot. From the seed, a flower grows, and inside the flower there's a little girl: Thumbelina.

But one night a fat toad hops into the room and steals the little girl away to a lake, to marry her to her ugly toad son. Some fish take pity on the girl and eat the stem of the waterlily leaf where Thumbelina is held prisoner. Then, all by herself, the girl drifts across the water on the leaf.

Winter comes, and Thumbelina is freezing and starving. In a hole in the ground, she finds a half-frozen swallow and nurses it back to health. Out of gratitude, the swallow flies her in spring to a warm land in the south.

There the girl meets a fairy prince with wings who is as tiny as she. They fall in love and get married. In the end the handsome flower elf gives her not only a pair of wings but a new name, too: Maya.

Then they fly off together to explore the world.

I close the book of fairy tales.

The realization is as painful as a red-hot stove door. It wasn't the wondrous story I didn't understand.

But the language.

I saw Mother opening her mouth and talking to me, but her words didn't make any sense. The strange phrases coming from her lips sounded oddly harsh and clipped.

Mother was speaking German. She read me the fairy tale to teach me her foreign language. Me, little Elly Watson from England who they'd kidnapped from the beach.

I can hardly breathe.

Dazed, I put the book down on my bedside table and push the window open. Closing my eyes, I take a deep breath. Who are the people in this house? I lean out of the window, sticking my head into the cold night. Is Boy really my brother? Is that his real name? Why did they snatch me?

Breathe, breathe, breathe.

Something heavy makes a dull thud against the wall. Luca's *cellulare* in my pocket. I have to hide it. Right now.

My eyes scour the room. I could slide it under the mattress, I think. But that's too risky, as Mother might change the bed out of the blue. Normally that's my job, but you never know. She might want to give me a nice surprise or reckon I'm too weak for housework at the moment. I mean, she thinks I'm ill because I'm not eating anything. To be honest, I still don't feel hungry, but I ought to have some porridge at breakfast, a few spoonfuls, at least. Mother mustn't get suspicious. I swallow. Even the thought of food makes me feel sick.

In the drawer of my bedside table, under the pile of books,

amongst the erasers and my favorite pencils—now that might be a safe hiding place. In an emergency, the *cellulare* would be within reach, and I could inform Luca in an instant.

No: too dangerous. Twice now Boy has borrowed a pencil from me without asking. I dread to think what would happen if he found Luca's little case and went running to Father with it.

The alarm clock shows 3:02 a.m.

Putting my hand in my pocket, I stroke the cool, glass surface with my fingertips. Where would be best to hide you? My black lucky stone, which is also in my pocket, rolls against my hand. I turn to the wardrobe. Of course: my secret treasure chest.

I open the doors to the wardrobe and kneel on the hard wooden floor. Pushing my wellies, sleeping bag, and *Grimms' Fairy Tales* to one side, I take out the colorful cigar box. When I open the lid, I'm met by the familiar scent of cedarwood and damp moss. I quickly bury the shiny black thing amongst the stones and the rare swan mussel I found on the shore, then close the lid. Now I just need to neatly arrange the sleeping bag and my doll Mirabell on top, and push it into the far corner. Done.

I'm suddenly overcome by exhaustion.

I lie down on the bed and close my eyes.

15

Mother's in the kitchen, cooking. The entire house smells of blueberry cake. That's unusual, I think. Mother doesn't normally bake until the afternoon. I wander over to her. How long have I slept? Without saying a word, Mother opens the firebox and puts in another couple of logs, even though it's blazing away in there. I look around, puzzled. Boy and Father are nowhere to be seen, even though my brother is always the first to come racing into the kitchen when he smells the wonderfully sweet aroma.

"Where are the others?" I ask.

Mother doesn't respond.

I stand right beside her, but Mother doesn't seem to take any notice. I look at the empty work surface. No whisk, no mixing bowl—everything is clean and tidy. As if she'd just magicked the cake dough. I tug on her apron strings until she finally turns to me.

"What were you thinking of?" she says, looking deadly serious.

At a loss as to what she's talking about, I give an uncertain shrug. Mother points at the oven door. I lean forward and peer through the yellowy-brown glass window. On the encrusted rack I see something slim, shiny, and black. I rack my brain and frown.

What's that?

"I found it in your room," Mother says, putting on a glove. Then she opens the oven door, releasing a horrible stench and black smoke. Mother waves her arms until the smoke dissipates. Then I realize what's in there: Luca's *cellulare*.

"Were you going to use it to talk to your parents, Elly?" Mother shouts, hysterical. "Well then, Elly, do it!" Grabbing me under the arms, she pushes me into the oven as if I were as light as a loaf of bread. I flail my arms and legs, trying to grab hold of the red-hot oven door, but it's hopeless. Mother shoves me all the way in, then she slams the metal door shut and starts laughing wildly. I thrash around, trying desperately to escape from my fiery metal grave. I scream for help, call Luca's name, but it's too late.

The flames devour my bones.

I open my eyes.

Mother is leaning over me, her hand on my forehead. "You're really hot," she says, shaking her head. "Maybe you ought to stay in bed today, Juno,"

"It was just a bad dream," I stammer, sitting up. I feel hot, unbelievably hot; my hair is stuck to my cheeks. Take a deep breath, Juno. In and out. I'm just about to pull off the duvet when I catch sight of the other side of the room, my wardrobe.

The doors are open.

Oh, no. The little black case.

Mother pushes me back onto the mattress. "No arguments, you're going to rest now." She points at the closed window. "What were you thinking, Juno?" Again she shakes her head, this time looking more serious. "You slept with the window open all night." She pulls the dark-blue material right up to my chin. "You were chilled to the bone when I came to wake you for breakfast. I had to fetch the sleeping bag to stop you from freezing."

I look down. Spread across my duvet is my blue winter sleeping bag from the wardrobe.

"It was just a nightmare, Mother," I say. "Just a dream. Anyway, it's summer. I don't need two layers."

"Who's Luca?" Mother asks all of a sudden.

I stiffen.

"You were calling out his name in your sleep."

With a shrug I pull off the covers and sit back up on the mattress. "I can't remember," I lie. As if on cue, my right forefinger begins to tremble, the throbbing gets stronger and I can't keep it under control. Panicked, I ball my fist and put on my slippers. "Luca?… Oh, yes, Mother. He was…um…he was one of the strangers who came to kill us. It was horrible, Mother."

"Where are you going?" she asks as I get up.

"To have a shower."

"OK, but after that you're having breakfast, Juno. Or are you still not hungry?"

"I'm ravenous," I reply quickly, pulling the spotted dressing-gown out of the wardrobe and shutting the doors.

"That's good to hear," Mother says, following me out onto the landing. When we're outside the bathroom she grabs my hand. "We'll be waiting for you down in the kitchen," she says, smiling. "Father's back on his feet, too."

I shudder.

"I'll hurry," I say, wrenching myself free and dashing into the bathroom.

Soon afterward I'm at the breakfast table with them, shoveling warm porridge into my mouth. I look at their lifeless faces. The whole family is assembled, and nobody is saying a word. Boy reaches for the large china bowl in the middle of the table and ladles more into his bowl. As if he hadn't eaten anything in days. Then I watch Mother pour elderflower syrup onto the strawberries in the bowl I made for Father's fifty-seventh birthday.

A Tuesday morning like any other, I think, trying to gulp down the slimy porridge as inconspicuously as possible. An almost intimate family tableau, since Father's started eating with us again in the kitchen.

I wish he wouldn't sit at the table without a top on.

Beads of sweat stick to his hairy chest.

Why hasn't he put a shirt on? I look away and gaze instead at the bowl of porridge in front of me—there's no better sight. I tell myself that the reason for this inappropriate display is that he wants us to see his bloodstained bandages. And keep at the front of our minds the evil strangers who supposedly are waiting on the other side of the lake.

But I know better.

"Does it still hurt, Father?" I ask, breaking the silence. Surprised, he looks down and shakes his head. Then he goes on eating.

Still nobody's talking.

The clatter of the crockery is maddening. To stop myself from having a fit, I strain to listen to the singing of the birds, warbling through the open kitchen window. Who are these people I've spent the last thirteen years of my life with?

Take a deep breath, Juno, nice and calm, now.

Once again I'm dogged by this strange turmoil I felt the first time I met Luca. Not knowing where I belong, where my heart lies. But now the feeling is different.

I'm a stranger. In my own family.

When we've finished washing up, I sit with Boy on the sofa, stare out of the open sitting room window, and listen to the piano in the recording play the Prelude in F Major. I've put on one of my favorite records, Claude Debussy's *Suite bergamasque*, to escape the tense silence. The familiar crackle of the record player is calming. A cool summer wind caresses my cheeks. It smells of damp grass.

I close my eyes and collect my thoughts.

Father's gone back up to his room for a rest; Mother's having a shower. I focus on every single sound. It helps me think.

I hear Father's plodding footsteps in the bedroom above. He seems to be wandering around aimlessly. Did he really row to the other side on Monday to kill Uncle Ole? To be honest, that's really hard to imagine. The ceiling creaks. All our lives, Father has taught us to respect every living creature. Perhaps it was an accident, and Uncle Ole had an unfortunate fall. Onto a tree stump, headfirst.

No: there was a knife. Luca said so. And Father's glasses were beside the body. I can't think of a logical explanation for that. When I press my eyelids together, I see red threads of light in the darkness before me. Father can't be a murderer.

My thoughts are going around and around. Faster and faster, in a circle. Juno, Father isn't *your* Father.

A roaring, gurgling noise: water flowing through the old pipes. Mother's in the shower.

How long did she sit beside my bed, watching me? Did I give away more in my dream than Mother has said? I hope not.

The steadfast ticking of the antique clock to my right. With every second, the ticking grows louder. How long will it be before Luca gets in touch?

Tick, tick. Tock. Tick, tock.

Was I really kidnapped in Italy as a child? Or is this just one of the strangers' vile tricks to make me trust Luca? I don't have much time to discover the truth.

Even though I know for certain that I didn't understand German at the time, I feel torn. Who can I still trust? My parents or Luca, a boy I don't know?

I'd love to be able to talk to Boy about this. Consult with him as to what we should do now. Find a solution and make the right decision. But that's too dangerous.

I'm on my own.

"Are you sick?" asks a voice from far away, while a thin finger digs into my ribs.

I wrench open my eyes in shock and turn around. Boy, sitting cross-legged on the sofa, is staring at me cynically. Then he shuts his nature book noisily. Excessively so.

"No," I say, brushing a loose strand away. My hair is sticking to my skin.

"What's wrong with you, then?"

"Could you keep a lookout for a sec?" I ask, ignoring his question.

I leap up and thrust both of my hands in the front pocket of my dress. Ready to lie. But Boy doesn't ask any questions. He just raises his eyebrows. It feels like minutes.

Eventually he nods with a mischievous grin on his face. He probably thinks this is some sort of game.

Without saying a word, he follows me into the hall. We stop by the stairs. I look up, and can still hear the shower running and footsteps coming from Father's room. I step forward and stand by the closed door next to the kitchen.

"What are you doing?" Boy whispers.

I point at Father's study. I need to find out whether Luca told the truth.

Boy looks wide-eyed and he hops from one foot to the other. "The library? That's not allowed! The commandments, Juno! We'll be severely punished!"

"I know," I reply, already holding the handle.

I press it down.

16

I enter the forbidden room, which smells of rotting wood, musty carpet, and sweet aftershave. The shutters in Father's library are closed; barely any light seeps in through the narrow slats revealing threads of dust in the air. I go past the desk and make straight for the shelves that run the length of the wall. That's where Mother's much-loved *Juliette* novels are. My eyes immediately pick out the first in the series, *The Love of My Life*. The one I tore a page from. The reason why we're no longer allowed in here.

Or at least that's what I thought all these years. Until now.

I see the old photo albums on the bottom shelf, twelve of them, at least. I'd taken a few of these out on that occasion, too, completely at random, the ones with the nicest covers. I had neatly piled the colorfully patterned albums on the desk in front of me, but then I'd thought I'd rather read the opening chapter of the *Juliette* novel.

Until Father had suddenly come in.

The blood drained from his face when he'd seen me sitting at the desk. He didn't say a word. I apologized for having torn the page, as sincerely as possible, but to no avail. He came marching over, grabbed me with his strong hand, and dragged me out of his study by my hair.

I touch the back of my head and feel the stinging pain again. How could I have been so gullible? Father wasn't furious because I'd torn the page of a book. No, it was the photo albums on the desk in front of me that had made him so mad.

I turn to Boy, who's still keeping watch in the doorway. Kneading his hands, he glances up the stairs, then back at me. His forehead is covered in beads of sweat.

"Hurry up, Juno!" he urges. I turn back to the shelves. Try to remember which albums I took out back then.

They're not labeled. No names, no dates.

It's pointless, my memories are dark and hazy, like a huge storm cloud in my mind. So at random, I pick a dark-brown leather one. I rapidly leaf through the thick card pages. Tiny black-and-white photographs of old men and women in hats. On a farm with a horse.

I turn another page.

A family in a cramped sitting room, lined up like a painting. An old man on a chair with white hair and long beard. Next to him are two girls in white dresses, behind them a woman in black with a veil over her face.

I keep going.

Two narrow mounds of earth, side by side; behind them two wooden crosses and two bouquets of flowers. Graves? Why did someone take a photo of them?

Puzzled, I look at the following pages. More bearded men in black suits, then a sleeping baby. Women in old-fashioned clothes, little boys in funny hats, girls in knee-length skirts, horse-drawn carriages, cows, spartan dining rooms.

Nobody is smiling. They all stare with serious expressions, their lips formed into narrow slits, almost in reproach. As if they knew I was doing something wrong.

I shut the leather photo album and put it tidily back on the shelf.

"What the hell are you doing in there?" Boy says, sounding agitated. I put my finger up to my lips; he rolls his eyes and shuts up. The next album I take out has a coarse orange felt cover, which is scratchy.

I open the album in the middle.

The color photo shows a young woman in a bright-yellow summer dress with black curly hair tied into two neat plaits. She's laughing. Around her neck is a chain with a silver cross, and she's carrying a brown briefcase under her arm. It looks like she's only a few years older than me. A few meters behind her, between two trees, towers a sand-colored, fairy-tale palace with decorated columns and stone angels on the curved window arches. What is that strange building?

I pick up the magnifying glass that's in a leather holder on Father's desk.

Now I can make out every detail. On the roof of the imposing castle is a half-naked statue, probably stone or marble. It's a bearded, muscular man swinging a sharp sword above his head. Below him, at his feet, two kneeling children are anxiously holding on to his legs. They're terrified of the hissing dragon right beside them. My eyes wander down to the blackish-green, gleaming metal sign with only one word in capital letters: VERITATI. Must be the name of the palace, I think, putting the magnifying glass back on the desk.

There's something handwritten beneath the photograph:

First semester, pharmacy, 1983
Julius Maximilian University, Würzburg

I turn the page to the next photo. A tiny attic room with barely any space for furniture. A desk, a chair, a bed, a wardrobe, a flowery rug. By the round attic window, through which you can see red autumnal leaves, the same young woman is sitting on a radiator, a big pile of books on her lap. She's smiling.

To the right of the photograph someone has written:

A free thinker does not stay where chance has pushed him
Heinrich von Kleist

My curiosity piqued, I keep looking.

The next photographs show her in a hall full of books, set on two floors, then on an old stone bridge that spans a wide river. In the background you can see the pointed towers of a castle. Another photo shows her sitting on a park bench in the arms of an older woman and a white-haired man with a walking stick, holding an ice-cream cone.

Parents visiting, Würzburg, 1983

All three of them are giving me a contented, almost proud smile.

The other two pages have color photos of the white-haired couple, with various backgrounds, mostly highly ornate churches. Then the young woman on her own again in her attic room in the light of a desk lamp. Through the window you can see snow on the trees.

She seems to like reading.

"Juno, what's taking so long?" Boy hisses so loudly that I flinch. "Father's going to kill us if he finds us in here!"

"One sec," I say, returning to the album and turning another page.

Two years pass: *1984* and *1985* are written by hand beneath the colorful photos. In these the young woman is wearing only pastel-colored silk blouses and ankle-length pleated skirts in matching colors.

Then the next page: a group photo, again in front of the fairy-tale palace with the hissing dragon. Blue sky, sun shining. The men are wearing dark suits, the women long, bright summer dresses. They've all got a white piece of paper that they proudly hold above their heads. I look more closely at the picture and search for the young woman. But I can't find her anywhere. There are too many faces, and the image is too blurry. Underneath, in handwriting:

1st pharmaceutical exam (PH1)
Interim certificate, Würzburg, 1985
Only TWO more years of grinding until finals!

I hurriedly turn the page. The same year. A large color photo that takes up almost half the page. And then I see her again, the young woman who loves reading.

Only four months later.

But she seems strangely different.

No silk blouse, no pleated skirt, no plaits.

Almost all of her black curly hair has been shaved off, especially on the left-hand side. What remains is streaked with blond. A huge gold earring dangles down to her shoulder.

Confused, I squint and put my face closer to the picture. This woman looks familiar somehow, now that her face is so much older and harsher.

Those broad nostrils. The piercing blue eyes. And the high cheekbones, pointed chin. I swallow.

It's her. Mother. It really is.

Instead of a modest pleated skirt she's now wearing an unusually short leather skirt with a zebra pattern. Bright-pink lipstick and her spotted shirt is unbuttoned to her breasts. You can even see her black bra straps.

Her fingers have green nails, and there's a thin white tube between them. It's glowing red and steaming.

Right beside her is a young man in chunky glasses with a fluffy mustache and reddish-blond, shoulder-length hair. He has his arm around her. Could that be Father?

The man is grinning, and his eyes look oddly glassy. He's wearing a shabby black leather jacket decorated with silver rivets. In his left hand is a green bottle, in his right he's also got a burning tube between his fingers. His nails are ragged and dirty.

Around them are other young people, likewise dressed in strange clothes. The dark room looks like a cellar, with unplastered walls and colorful balloons hanging everywhere.

Beneath the color photo is written:

New Year's Eve, Hamburg, 1985

With a little heart beside it.

I scrutinize this photo a while longer, then leaf forward the next few pages, taking in the captions:

First flat together, St. Pauli, Feb 1986
Motorbike tour, Easter '86
Summer holiday in the Black Forest
Move to Salzgitter, October 1986

Mother and Father are in most of the photos. They look happy. But the older, white-haired couple aren't in any of the pictures anymore.

Next page.

Mother sitting at the window of a tiny square house, not bigger than a shoebox, surrounded by colorful papers and magazines. Above is a glowing sign in capital letters, KIOSK. There's another of those little smoking sticks between her lips. Outside the open window, Father in a leather jacket giving the thumbs-up. Mother isn't smiling.

First job, 1986. Grateful

I spin around to Boy, who's still staring upstairs and doesn't realize I'm looking at him. He appears focused; I can rely on him.

OK, the next pages.

Move, May 1987, Lindenfels, Odenwald

Now a photo of Father standing in a well-lit hall with floor-to-ceiling frosted windows. He's wearing blue overalls with a golden zipper, which are covered in dark stains. He's holding something silver in his hand and smiling at the camera. Hovering above his head is a green vehicle with four wheels.

Werner workshop, 1987
Nibelungenstrasse. Finally!

Mother in an empty, unplastered room. On the wall a wooden cross. Through the murky windowpanes, you can make out an old tree in a field with a few yellowy-brown leaves still clinging to it. On the floor of the corner room, lots of brown cardboard boxes, some stacked on top of each other, as well as three wooden chairs, a blue-checkered sofa, and a round table.

I'm surprised when I look at Mother; she's gotten fatter. Her cheeks are rosy, and her black hair comes down to her shoulders again. She's wearing a baggy red summer dress with white spots and a light-gray cardigan over it. Her hands together, as if in prayer, are clutching her huge belly, which sticks out from her body like a balloon.

Lo, children are an heritage of the Lord:
and the fruit of the womb is his reward. (Psalm 127, Verse 3)
November 1987—37 weeks

There's another little heart beneath this.

"Come out now, Juno! Mother'll be here any minute!" Boy mutters, his voice cracking. Sensing his panic in his voice, I turn to give him a stern look. Boy is waving his arms around and pointing at the stairs: "The water! She's turned the shower off!"

"OK!" I call back. "I'm almost done!"

I stare at the picture again, at Mother's huge belly. The expression of delight on her face. Then I inquisitively turn the page.

It's empty. No photo.

I keep turning: one, two, three, five, ten pages. But all the rest of the album is as white as snow. No photos, no handwritten text. Finally I get to the end of the album where there's nothing, either. There must be at least twenty empty pages.

Strange, I think, putting the album back on the shelf. Then a thin piece of paper flaps to the floor. It must have slipped from the album.

I pick it up: an article cut out of a newspaper. But I only recognize the woman in the picture when I look more closely. It's Mother. Wrinkled skin and big bags under her eyes. Not a flattering photo. Like a china doll, she stares into the distance coldly and stiffly. No smile, not even the hint of a grin. I read the headline: Spectacular Escape from Odenwald Psychiatric Clinic—Violent Patient Still on the Loose.

Patient? Was Mother ill? What is *psychiatric*? I've never heard of it. At a loss, I put the newspaper cut-out back into the album and reach for the next one.

The mint-green volume is on the very far right of the shelves. It appears to be the newest album. At least that's the impression I get from the spine. I take it out and put it on my lap. There are various childish images on the shiny plastic cover: a tree, two birds, a rainbow, a laughing sun, and a bear in a hat on a red bicycle. On a yellowed sticker, I can recognize Mother's handwriting: *Book of Consolation*.

I want to open the album, but a tiny lock keeps it shut. Annoyed, I tug at the thin plastic strap, but it's firmly attached to the book. An unfamiliar combination of anger, disappointment, and curiosity wells inside me. Without much thought, I reach for the scissors on Father's desk. Squeezing hard, it takes me two goes to cut through the strap.

I put the scissors back and turn to the first page.

2006

That's nineteen years later.

A square photo with a thick white frame. A grainy photo of Mother in the mountains. She's standing by a beautiful river with dark sunglasses perched on her nose. It's pouring with rain. A few meters behind her, beneath the snow-covered chain of mountains, you can see a group of between ten and fifteen boys and girls at the edge of a forest. All are wearing raincoats and carrying small backpacks on their backs.

Directly below this, the next square photo, also taken from a distance, shows two girls putting up a tent beside the river. The sun shines down on the mountains from a blueberry-colored sky. A thick red circle has been drawn above the head of the girl on the left.

Eienwäldli Campsite, Engelberg, Switzerland, 2006

I turn the page.

Another photo. The same girl, this time on a flowery mattress. Her eyes peacefully closed. Dim light slants in through the curtains of the compact dining room, which scarcely has enough space for two adults. What kind of weird, cramped place is that? You can see the mountains through the narrow window. Jotted beneath the photo, it says:

Ruth, about 6, 2006

There's a rustling when I quickly turn the page. A newspaper clipping, stuck into the album. It shows the sleeping girl in the photo. Above it, in big letters:

Girl abducted from campsite!

I swallow.

"Juno, she's coming!" Boy suddenly exclaims, almost in a panic. "Get out, quick! Mother's on the stairs!" I turn to him; his face is as white as the wall.

My heart is racing.

"Boy, what are you doing?" I hear Mother bark from the stairs. My brother gives a start, then points at the window behind me with his trembling hands.

"Nothing," he says, slamming the door to the study.

17

Pressing the album to my chest I look around the room. Have I got time to climb out of the window? Or would it be better to hide? Mother will be at the door in seconds. I don't think my brother can stop her from opening it. Especially as Mother must have seen him waving with his hands. How's he going to try to explain that? Or was she too far away to notice? My eyes alight on the green farmhouse cupboard on the opposite side of the room.

I hurry over and am already gripping the wooden handle.

"You weren't in Father's room, were you?" I can hear Mother's voice loud and clear; she must be right beside the door.

Frantically I pull at the cupboard door.

Locked!

"No, Mother," Boy replies. It sounds a bit too put-on.

"So why did you shut the door?"

"It was open."

"Really?"

I swiftly hitch up my skirt at the back and stick the narrow album into my knickers. The cover sticks to my skin and feels cold. But the album is too heavy, and my knickers slide down.

The door handle moves.

I gasp, then instinctively leap forward and lean against the wall beside the door. Pressing my arms and back against the wood paneling, I try to keep the album in place with my pelvis. I mustn't move!

The door flies open, coming to a stop right in front of my nose. I hold my breath as I hear Mother enter the dark library.

"What were you looking for in here?"

"Nothing, Mother."

"Where's your sister?"

"I...I don't know," Boy replies, standing in the doorway. "Maybe on the big rock outside?"

Mother prowls through the library, her footsteps heavy and even. Peeking through the narrow bright gap between the frame and the door, I can make out the silhouette of my brother, rubbing his brow with his sleeve.

"You know what will happen if you're lying, don't you?"

Boy says nothing. More heavy footsteps in the room. Mother's heels on the hard wooden floor sound like thunderbolts. A window is jerked open.

The startled flapping of birds outside the window makes me jump. I press my lips together so I don't scream. A cool draft wafts into my hiding place behind the door, brushing my hot cheeks.

Stay calm, Juno, breathe.

Then it's silent. All I can hear is the chirping of the crickets in the reeds. Mother scans the garden, the shore, and the big rock for me.

Please, dear God, let her go out again.

"Juuuuno!" Mother calls out to the lake. "Juuuuno?"

No response. Of course not.

"Come back into the house right now!" Her voice sounds like a raging winter storm. "Do you hear me? Right now!"

I can feel the sharp photo album sliding down, taking my knickers with it. In a panic I push my wet back against the wall. But it doesn't help.

My knickers slide further and further down.

"I could go and look for her," Boy says quietly, taking a few steps into Father's study.

Sweat is dripping down my forehead. I press myself against the wall as hard as I can, spreading my legs, stretching my panties to stop the album from slipping further. Bending my torso forward carefully, I try to reach the hem of my knickers with my fingertips.

The window shuts with a loud crash and it's immediately dark again. Mother comes closer and stops a meter away from the door. I can hear her breathing—she's whooshing like a steam locomotive.

A tense silence.

She seems to be contemplating Boy's suggestion.

Finally I'm touching the hem of my panties and I pinch the thin material between my thumb and index finger, which are slippery. I won't be able to keep hold of my knickers for long. My heart is in my mouth.

"You've got fifteen minutes to find her," Mother says finally, pushing Boy out of the room. "Juno is sick. She should be in bed!"

The door slams shut, sending a gust of air whirling around my nose. I stand there motionless in Father's warm, stuffy library, legs apart, back pressed up against the wall, my fingertips on my knickers. Breathing regularly, in and out.

And I wait, I wait for them to go away. But they're still on the other side of the closed door. What are they spending so long talking about?

I can't hold onto the book forever. At any moment it's going to crash to the floor. Please, Boy, get Mother away from the door, I pray over and over again. Get her far away from here. My entire body is cramping up, I can feel the thin material slipping from my clammy fingertips, I press them together more tightly. No, don't!

Then I suddenly hear a key in the lock.

It's turned twice.

I haven't heard either of their voices for five minutes now. Putting my ear to the door I listen one last time.

No footsteps, no talking, just an unnerving silence.

Cautiously I press the handle; it is indeed locked. I'm locked in. I press the album more tightly to my chest. That was close. I've got a few minutes at most to get out of here unnoticed. So Boy doesn't get punished. Only because *I* broke our third commandment, and my brother helped me. What were you thinking, Juno? You're the older one.

Annoyed, I turn to face Father's desk and let my eyes roam the entire dark room. I'm going to have to escape into the garden through the window. There's no other way out. But which window? The left-hand one leads straight to the kitchen window, the right-hand one to our front door. I creep to the middle of the room and readjust my panties. The elastic is knackered. It was a stupid idea to stick the album in them.

I'm just about to make for the right-hand window—on this side of the house there's a thicket of elderflower and two stout pine trees, when I notice Father's magnifying glass on the polished desk. Oh no! I was in such a hurry I forgot to put it back in the pen holder. Thank goodness Mother didn't notice.

I cross myself and put the magnifying glass back in its rightful place. When I go over to the window, I feel the heat seeping through the narrow slits in the shutters. I fiddle with the tiny lock on the window and venture a furtive glance into the garden. Please, God, let nobody be watching me. The mint-green photo album lands open on the grass. I put one leg after the other over the narrow sill, climb through the opening, and drop briskly onto the sandy ground.

A stabbing pain. Gritting my teeth, I sweep the gravel from my knee. Luckily, it's not bleeding. I glance around: nobody to be seen. Not even Boy. A black bird squawks and flutters above my head. I jump.

Closing the shutters, I pick up the album and steal down to the shore. The sun burns my shoulder. I need to find a safe place to keep the book so I can keep studying it tonight, undisturbed. Besides, it's evidence if Boy refuses to believe me. I need to get the lowdown on *Ruth*, that girl. Could she be my dead sister? Was she kidnapped, too?

Halfway to the lake, my elder sister's grave still in sight, I think of the tool shed. I could hide the album in one of the crates or toolboxes, where it would be safe from the rain. I run from birch to pine, ducking from shrub to bush, always with one eye on our cabin. There's no movement at the windows, as if the house were sleeping. It stands there silently and eerily between the tall trees.

I run faster until I finally get to the old well and flop down on the grass. I check all around me one last time, stick my head carefully above the wall then hurry straight to the red shed, my hair lashing my face. After a few leaps and bounds, I yank open the rotten wooden door and enter the dark space.

I'm met by a stale heat that sticks to my face and body like a wet towel. It's hard to breathe in here. It smells of warm varnish and paint, and damp moss. A weak light filters through the yellowish-white embroidered curtains. Exhausted, I shut the shed door behind me and put my hands on my thighs. I made it.

Looking around, I see floor-to-ceiling shelves filled with wooden boxes, garden tools, paint pots, and piles of lounger cushions. I shuffle deeper into the abyss of the shed. Where can I hide the album? Where is Father least likely to look? I even glance up at the roof, which is covered in a shimmer of spiderwebs. Maybe on one of the wooden beams? People don't often look up. But then I catch sight of the dusty, silver metal box. Boy's fishing gear. A safe place. During the week, only he and I open this box. Mother only does it on Sundays when she makes fishcakes.

I pull the heavy box off the shelf, set it on the floor and open the metal clasp. Two reels, a ball bearing, a long cast spool, more than twenty hooks and swivels, five rolls of tackle, stoppers, beads, a small landing net, floats, and other stuff we need for fishing.

I push it all to one side to bury the album underneath. But before that, I want to take another quick look. I open it.

The square photo of the sleeping girl.

Ruth, about 6, 2006

Then the newspaper clipping.

Girl abducted from campsite!

I keep reading.

Large numbers of Swiss police in the canton of Obwalden and the neighboring cantons of Bern, Nidwalden, and Uri are searching for a missing girl. On Sunday, six-year-old Ruth F. from Liestal disappeared from a campsite in Engelberg, Switzerland.

The police are not ruling out the possibility of a crime. According to a police spokesperson, Ruth had been playing with a friend by the river at the campsite and was heading back to the camp counselors in the afternoon. On the short way back, the child disappeared. The only trace of Ruth is a yellow tracksuit top found by one of the search teams on an embankment. The police began their search for the girl in caravans and holiday cottages. "We cannot rule out the possibility that the girl is being hidden or detained somewhere," the spokesperson said. More than 200 police officers have been combing the mountains, while divers and dogs have also been deployed.

So far there has been no sign of the girl.

When I turn the page, I shudder.

The next photograph was taken on our island; I immediately recognize the big rock by the shore. Ruth, the kidnapped girl, is standing by the water in a flowery dress, looking gloomily at the camera, her thin, pale arms hanging limply. Underneath, in Mother's handwriting:

Our first daughter, May 2007
Plus side: Ruth has finally settled in
Minus side: still suffering from homesickness and loneliness

I bring the album closer to my face; the blurred photo has faded at the edges. Not only the girl but Ruth's summer dress seems strangely familiar. Of course! She's wearing my much-loved flowery dress I got as a surprise present for my seventh birthday. Have I been wearing Ruth's old clothes? The realization strikes me like an adder bite.

Ruth was my big sister! She was the first one they abducted!

Suddenly the shed door is jerked open behind me, an excruciating screech of metal and wood. In shock I drop the album into the fishing box.

"For God's sake, Juno! What are you doing here?"

I anxiously shut the lid and turn to face the door. Boy is standing there, hands on hips, his face as pale as flour.

"I was just checking our fishing gear."

"Fishing's canceled today," he says. "Because of you."

I push the metal box back onto the shelf and brush the spiderwebs from my hands. The album should be safe there till next Sunday.

"What were you doing in Father's library?" Boy takes a step toward me and grabs my shoulders. "Can you explain that?" He squeezes more tightly, I feel a slight pain, but I don't move a muscle.

"I can't talk about it. Not yet," I reply, looking at Boy's hands on my shoulders. "It's too dangerous for both of us."

I can see him straining to think. He puts his arms down and cocks his head. "Were you reading Mother's mushy love stories again? Those kissy-kissy books?"

I nod sheepishly.

"I knew it!" Boy laughs, slapping his thigh. Then he turns serious again. "And for that you'd risk us both being locked in the safe room? Are you mad?"

"I'm sorry," I whisper, grateful that my twelve-year-old brother is so gullible.

"No, Juno, that's not good enough. Not this time." He points a finger at me. "You owe me one."

I'd love to tell him everything. That I didn't run this risk for selfish reasons. Not because of some silly romance. But if I tell Boy the truth too early, the truth about Mother and Father, Ruth, and me, I could put Luca's rescue plan in danger. And probably our lives, too.

Boy could never keep a secret.

"We ought to go now," I say instead, pushing my brother out of the shed and closing the door behind us. The sun is blinding. I sneak a glance at my sister's grave. A long-beaked pigeon is sitting on her cross, preening itself. Finally I know your name, I think, hoping that Ruth is now in a nicer place.

We don't say a word the rest of the way back.

When we get to the cabin, Father's waiting for us, blocking the back door. He stands there, legs apart and frowning. Pearls of sweat stick to his cheeks that are as red as a lobster. He spits out each word individually: "Juno! Where the hell were you?"

I fumble around for an excuse, but can't think of anything and my right forefinger begins to twitch.

I yank my hand behind my back.

Too late: Father noticed.

18

Grabbing my arm, he drags me into the kitchen, throws me onto a chair, and slams the door shut. Father plants himself in front of me, as massive as an angry gorilla, and pounds his fist on the table. I wince.

"Juno's sick," I hear Boy's timid voice behind Father.

"You stay out of this!"

"Please don't be so harsh on her."

"Where were you, Juno?" Father sways as he bends down to me, propping his arms on the table. His breath stinks of alcohol. I peer at the kitchen clock above the fridge. It's ten to eleven. In the morning.

Puzzled, his eyes follow mine, then he seems to read my mind. "It helps with the pain," he whispers, before slumping awkwardly on a chair beside me. His forearm goes crashing into the table. "Give me your right hand, Juno."

"No," I reply. "You're drunk."

"I'm not going to ask you again."

My arm shakes as I put it on the cold table. Leaning forward, Father stares at me. Burst blood vessels streak the whites of his eyes. Thin red worms in milk, I think.

"Where were you?"

My index finger wiggles in his hand.

"She was in the shed," Boy says, moving beside Father.

"Juno can speak for herself."

"In the shed, Father."

"She was just checking our fishing gear."

Father's hand flails backward, hitting Boy on the temple. Boy staggers and falls to the floor, the back of his head hitting the work surface and table leg. Two thuds, then he lies there motionless by Father's feet. I leap up from my chair, bend over him, and stroke his pale cheek. It's ice cold. My brother, his eyes wide open, looks at me and whispers, "I'm sorry, Juno."

"Don't move," I say. "Are you in pain?"

"Head." Boy's voice is the mere breath of a word, then he slumps unconscious.

Mother appears in the doorway. "What's going on here?"

"The boy stumbled," Father says, struggling up out of his chair. He peers down at us. "I warned him."

"Have you been drinking?" Mother asks cuttingly.

"No."

Kneeling beside Boy, she lays a hand on his brow and shakes her head in anger. "Haven't you learned anything? We need to think clearly and logically, now."

"Didn't mean to do it."

"He needs a doctor," I say. "Quickly!"

Shoving me to one side, Mother puts an arm around Boy's shoulder and gently lifts him up. She fans him with her left hand; her movements look ever more fretful.

"Can you hear me?" she says, her voice wobbling.

Boy opens his eyes and blinks. He lifts his head and his lips open only slightly. "What happened?"

"You passed out."

"You see, he's back on his feet," Father says, staggering to the kitchen door. He grabs onto the doorframe. "It was nothing."

"Boy needs to go to bed!" Mother screams at him. "He might have a concussion! Help me carry him upstairs!" Father turns to us, his eyes staring into space, then he nods silently.

I sit on Boy's mattress as he sleeps. Mother's given me the job of keeping a watch on my brother until she comes back and takes over the bedside vigil. He might fall unconscious again, which is typical with a concussion. She's put a bucket by the bed in case he throws up. Seeing as his eyes are closed, I don't know how I'm supposed to tell if he's lost consciousness again, but I don't take my eye off Boy for a minute. His chest rises weakly, then deflates like a balloon; he's wheezing like a pot of boiling water.

Mother's curses resound through the paper-thin wall in Father's bedroom. A glass smashes on the floor.

Then it goes quiet.

A door opens; I hear Mother's heels on the landing. Like thunderclaps getting ever closer. I turn to the door and wait for her to appear. Through the gap under the door, I can see her shadow.

The handle is pressed down, then the door swings open. She stands there in the doorway, hair standing up wildly, eyes swollen. She's smiling, but I sense it's forced. It looks fake and artificial.

"You can go now, Juno," she says, entering the room and standing beside the bed. "I'll take over now."

I get up and nod.

"I don't want you to leave your room again today," Mother says, laying a hand on my shoulder. It's hot and clammy. "Not until Boy's over the worst."

"Why did Father do that?"

She gives me a look of surprise.

"Boy was just trying to explain that I was in the tool shed checking our fishing gear," I say determinedly. I feel a tingle in my finger, but I really don't care now. I could explode. "He was only trying to be kind. I mean, I didn't know you were looking for me."

"Father can be unpredictable when he drinks. He's always been like that, I'm afraid. Ever since I've known him. But he was only worried because you'd suddenly disappeared, do you understand?" Mother points her chin at the door. "Now go!"

Only worried, I repeat in my head, trotting out of the room with my head bowed. The situation is becoming increasingly dangerous. Do they suspect anything? Why was Father drinking? What was the reason for it? I close the door silently behind me and look down the dark landing.

A chink of light slants through the open door to Father's room. I wonder what he's up to. Maybe I ought to put my head around the door.

As I creep past the bathroom, I hear Father trying to open a drawer. It seems to be stuck as he's tugging and shaking it. And swearing. When I get to his door, I lean forward and hazard a glance into the bedroom.

Father is standing with his back to me, still with no top on. His checkered shirt hangs over the back of a chair.

The drawer grates as it springs open. Father reaches inside and takes out a white bundle. Gauze.

His hands shaking, he unrolls the gauze and wraps it around his bare body, swaying as he turns, his head bowed. My eyes focus on his fleshy torso. Bewildered, I inspect his hairy torso for the cut that Mother stitched. But I can't see anything.

No wound, no scar, no stitches.

How's that possible? Father is unscathed. So why the bandaging?

Tiptoeing back to my room, I collapse on the bed in exhaustion and watch the shadow play of the birch leaves dancing on the ceiling. Suddenly I understand. I see it all quite clearly in my head. I shiver and pull the duvet over my legs.

That wasn't Father's blood in the rowing boat but Uncle Ole's. Father can wrap the gauze around his tummy as many times as he likes to keep up his false pretense; my last doubts have now gone. Luca's suspicions were right. Father waited in the woods for Uncle Ole, because I'd been seen at the kitchen window. Me, the missing girl whose picture has appeared in all the papers. Father followed him across the lake and stabbed him to death. Sneakily, quickly, and painlessly. To prevent him from notifying the guards. But Father was too late. The old postman had already sent my picture to Luca's *capo*. Even so, on Monday Father pretended to be annoyed as he waited for the paper. He knew that Uncle Ole would never come to see us on the island again.

Father, a cold-blooded killer.

I could weep. Thrash about. Scream.

But that would only attract Mother's attention. She'd come storming into the room and ask me why I was making such a noise.

I'd have to lie again, and she'd check my finger. There's too much of a risk that she'll force my secret out of me and that I'll tell the truth. About Luca's *cellulare* in my wardrobe.

That finger of mine—I *hate* it!

There's nothing else I can do. Furious, I turn onto my tummy, bury my face into the pillow and bellow the hopelessness of the situation out of my soul. Scream my worries into the dark depths of the pillow until in the end I start to cry.

Why me? What have I done?

Once I've wiped the tears from my eyes and tied my hair into a tight ponytail—so tight that my scalp hurts—I take heart again. Springing up off the bed, I open the wardrobe, put the colorful cigar box on the wooden floor in front of me, and flip open the lid.

The glass of the *cellulare* is jet black. Is it broken? I gasp. Has it all been in vain? Or does it work like our radio? I don't know because we're never allowed to touch Mother's kitchen radio. Trembling, I take the slim object out and examine every side. In our bunker, on the shelves of supplies with the preserves, Father collects all sorts of batteries for emergencies. Maybe…

As if my touch is magic, the glass starts flashing, and colorful squares appear on the surface. Above them some writing slides down. A message. From Luca. The corners of my mouth instinctively twitch upward into a smile.

Dear Elly. I'm wor...

But then the message suddenly disappears again. Where's it gone? I shake the device.

Nothing happens.

Bewildered, I turn the thing around and around. No buttons or switches. I search the glass surface, examine the little squares. And then I discover the green symbol with a speech bubble, above it a little red circle. With a number one. What does that mean?

It's very simple to use, Luca said. Maybe for him. Every fiber of my body is filled with despair. What should I do now? How do you use this thing? Nervously I rock back and forth.

Elly? Are you there?

Again a message pops down. No idea what I have to do. I wipe my brow. Why didn't Luca explain how this strange object works? I've just collected my thoughts when the second message disappears, too. As quickly as it arrived.

But now there's a little "2" beside the green symbol. The number in the red circle has changed.

How does it work? It's like witchcraft.

Astonished, I touch the number with my fingertip, like a sort of reflex. All of a sudden, the thing launches into an uncanny life of its own: the symbol immediately gets bigger, flies toward me, and fills the entire glass surface.

I drop the *cellulare* in shock.

It falls onto the wooden floor with a loud crash. I give a start and stare rigidly at the door to my bedroom. Hopefully Mother didn't hear the crash. Shaking myself from the shock, I pick up the box again and hide it in my lap.

Then I wait.

But Mother doesn't come.

No footsteps on the landing.

Relieved, I take hold of the *cellulare* and inspect the surface. A long list of names and round pictures. I recognize Luca instantly. He's smiling at me, and beside his face it says *Luca Conti (lavoro/polizia)*, with a small "2." I tap the number and a new picture immediately opens:

Luca's messages to me!

I've found them! The glass reacts to my touch. Proud to have worked it out all by myself, I begin to read:

Dear Elly, I'm worried about you. I hope you're OK. And your brother, too. Please get in touch when you read my message. And PLEASE watch out! Ciao, L.

My heart leaps.

Then a second message, right below.

Elly? Are you there?

Yes, I am! I really want to answer Luca. Tell him I miss him. But how? How can I send a reply? Maybe also with my finger. I tap the glass, and at once little letters appear from below as if the device were able to read my mind. Using my fingertip, I type my reply, letter by letter:

Dear Luca, Boy is unconscious. Father hit him. I miss you. When can you come and get us? Juno.

I stare at these few words. Has he already read my message? Then I see the little blue circle with the arrow beside my message. Do I have to press it?

The noise of an owl hooting in the night. It comes from the device. My message has been sent. I wait.

Less than a minute later, a new message appears on the glass. Luca has replied. As a precaution, I turn to the door again, but it's silent on the landing.

I'm alone. With Luca.

Hit? Are you in danger? Can we talk briefly?

I read his message a second time. A third time. How I'd love to hear his voice now. Right by my ear. But what if Mother or Father came in? It's too risky. They could be outside my door at any minute to check if I'm in bed like I've been told.

I could prepare for an emergency, however. Planning is one of my strengths. It just has to look convincing. And I've no time to lose. I put the cigar case back in the wardrobe and close the doors. I tiptoe into bed and slip beneath the duvet.

Then I reach for the book of fairy tales on my bedside table, open it in the middle, put the *cellulare* on the page and type my answer with a quivering finger:

Yes.

I wait.

No response.

I keep looking at the glass surface in anticipation, then at the door. But Luca doesn't reply.

Three minutes pass.

Did I write something wrong? Hasn't he received my message? I did press the blue arrow. I'm sure of that.

Suddenly the little case vibrates in my hands.

In danger? Or talk?

I shake my head at my stupidity; I ought to have written a longer message. My ambiguity has wasted precious minutes. Well done, Juno. He's probably really worried now and won't risk putting me in further danger. Concentrate!

Talk, I reply quickly.

In less than two seconds Luca's picture appears on the shiny surface, and beneath it a green circle with the word *Answer* on it. I press this with my finger and hold the little box up to my ear.

"Luca?" I whisper.

"Is everything alright? Can you talk?"

"Yes," I say, as my body is flooded by a warm shower. It feels so good to hear his voice. The familiar voice of a friend. I glance at the door.

"What happened, Elly? Where is your brother now?" Luca asks. I can hear the tension in his words, and I look again at the book of fairy tales in front of me. Thumbelina and the winged prince.

In the background, close to Luca, I can hear men's animated voices all talking at once in a foreign language.

"In his room," I say. "Mother's watching him."

"Can he be transported?"

"What do you mean?" I say, glancing again at the door.

"Is your brother badly injured?"

"I don't know. No, I don't think so."

"*Bene.*"

"When can you come to the island?"

A tense silence at the other end. I can hear Luca breathing. Then he speaks to another man in the room in a foreign language. They seem to be discussing something. Luca raises his voice. Then silence again.

"Luca?"

"Elly, *ti prego*. I can't talk for long," Luca whispers. "They don't know I'm speaking to you. But please listen, I need a precise description of your brother. Maybe I can find out which international missing person report might be him. How old is he now?"

"Boy is twelve."

"So he was abducted and taken to the island *after* you?" Luca says with a measure of hope in his voice. "How long ago was that?"

I mull over this question. I can't expressly remember a kidnapping. To be honest, over the last few years, I've never wondered about how Boy came to be with us on the island. He was just there one day. No, hold on. Boy wasn't just there. Father brought him back from a shopping trip.

"Elly, when was that? What year did your brother join you on the island?"

"When I was five," I reply, lost in thought, picturing Father's rowing boat in my mind. I can smell damp, freshly cut grass in front of the house. Mother in a green cardigan.

"So, ten years ago?"

"He spoke a different language?" I say quietly. "I didn't think anything of it. Father had just brought him home from the supermarket. It's so long ago."

"From the supermarket?" Luca sounds confused, then wide awake. "Elly, what language?"

I stare at the book of fairy tales open before me. At the picture of the ugly, fat toad that has taken Thumbelina away to the lake. The little girl has never seemed so familiar as now. "I…I don't know. Boy was only two. We were children." I turn to the window where a black bird flits past and whisper, almost begging him, "When can you come and get us, Luca?"

"Our team has discussed the rescue mission, Elly. Don't worry, we'll get you from the island soon. Our plan at the moment is to—"

The door to my room is thrust open. In a panic I drop the *cellulare* onto the book and shut it.

"Who were you talking to?" Her voice is icy as she comes into my room.

"You gave me a fright, Mother."

She approaches my bed slowly. Looks at me with narrowed eyes. Two fine lines on her face, as thin as the wrinkles on her brow.

"I was just reading out loud," I stammer, feeling the familiar pulse in my finger. "For Boy." Mother stands a pace away from me. She looks at me like I am a dangerous insect.

As discreetly as possible I turn to my bedside table and open the top drawer. "I thought I'd read to him from my book later on. So he doesn't get bored. He's all alone in his room."

"I'm here. And so is Father."

"Uh-huh," I reply, slipping the book into the drawer, which I casually push shut. I give her a smile. "Boy still likes me reading him fairy tales. Even though he's twelve."

"Your brother's asleep."

"I didn't know that."

"Show me your right hand, Juno."

"What?"

She sits on the bed and holds out her hand. I shake my head. Mother clenches her fist and opens it again. "Who were you talking to? And don't lie to me!"

I can smell her suppressed rage and the sourness of her stomach when she suddenly grabs my wrist and clasps it like a heavy iron bar.

I'm trapped. I look desperately for a way out.

Eventually I muster all my strength to free myself from her grasp, and I race out of the room.

"Where the hell are you going?" Mother shouts.

"To the toilet!" I call back without turning around. When I hear her jump up from my mattress, I start running.

Run down the dark, narrow landing.

Open the bathroom door, go to the sink, wrench on the tap, and run ice-cold water on my right index finger. It hurts. Fine pinpricks on my skin. But the finger is still twitching. It's going to give me away. Me, my lies, and Luca's little magic box. What am I doing? I scour the bathroom. How can I finally put an end to this treacherous twitching?

I hear a noise coming from my room: the crunching and grating of metal. Mother's pulled open the drawer of my bedside table! My heart's about to burst from my chest. Any second now she's going to take out the fairy-tale book. She'll open it and find the *cellulare* inside.

Then it'll all be over.

Boy and I will be finished.

I eye the open bathroom door. In a flash I'm beside it, staring at the massive hinge. Trembling, I jam my right forefinger into the narrow gap between the door and the frame. I feel the sharp wooden edges wedging my finger from both sides, like two blunt scissor blades pressing my skin all the way to the bones, which makes me think of father's vice in the tool shed. I close my eyes and grit my teeth. Sweat is running down my forehead.

I hold my breath.

And slam the door as hard as I can.

19

I scream, scream bloody murder, drowning out the crunching of my finger bones.

The pain shoots through my body, reaching every fiber of it, like glowing lava. Mother's agitated cries sound muffled, as if they were coming from miles away, from the other side of the lake. Everything is spinning.

I feel giddy; I have to sit. Bathed in sweat, I pull my broken finger out of the crack of the door and fall onto the tiles, curling up on the floor like a little baby. Mother's pink slippers appear in my eyeline, blurred, then her hands, her knee, her breasts. She bends right over me.

"Oh, no, Juno! What have you done?" Her voice sounds reproachful rather than concerned. As if I'd let the milk burn on the cooker.

I can't summon the strength to answer her; I just want to lie here in the bathroom. Alone. Huddled up in the hope that this agonizing pain will finally stop.

"What the hell happened?" Mother cries, slapping the tiles just a few centimeters from my nose. The noise of her wedding ring striking the ceramic floor is like a salvo from Father's rifle.

"Spit it out!"

When I still don't answer her, she slides closer on her knees and hisses angrily in my ear, "You're going to tell me right now what you did, or I'll stick you in the hole for two days!"

Shaking, I outstretch my right arm and hold my bloody forefinger up to her face. Now Mother screams, too, and claps a hand over her mouth. I feel sick when I see the finger for the first time. It's bent upward at a strange angle, as if it didn't belong to my hand.

"We need to get some ice on that right away!" Mother says, rushing out of the bathroom. She runs downstairs, presumably to the freezer.

This is my chance. Quick!

Supporting myself with my left hand, I use every ounce of my strength to push myself up. Once on my feet, I feel woozy again. My body begins to waver like a lone reed in the wind. Leaning against the doorframe, I close my eyes in exhaustion. Bad idea: it only feels worse, as if someone were mashing my innards with their fists. I teeter down the landing into my room and make for the bedside table.

The top drawer is half open.

Saved by a whisker, I think, crossing myself. With my left hand, I take out the book, chuck it onto the duvet, open it in the middle and breathe a sigh of relief. It's still there: Luca's *cellulare*. Grabbing the device, I scan the room.

Should I put it back inside the wardrobe?

Or is there a more secure hiding place?

I don't have much time for deliberation as I can already hear Mother trudging up the stairs.

She's on the landing.

I need to hurry. Instinctively I stuff the thing beneath my mattress, arrange the duvet, shut the book, and have just put it back in the drawer when Mother appears behind me. She's holding a jug of ice cubes, a pencil, and a roll of gauze bandage.

"Sit down, Juno," Mother instructs me, sounding strangely affectionate.

I sit on the bed and hold out my bent finger, which has now turned blue. Mother sits beside me and puts the jug on the bedside table, while her eyes fix on the half-open drawer. "Funny coincidence, isn't it, that it was your right index finger?" she says very calmly, as she reaches into the drawer and takes out my book.

Not knowing what to say, I just nod.

"If you like, I could read you something from this to cheer you up," she says, leafing through the book, then putting it on her lap. "Like I used to in front of the fire—remember?"

I nod again.

How could I forget? That's how she taught me this foreign language. I shudder; the pain in my finger seems to have abated for the moment.

"Once upon a time…" Mother says, smirking, "there was a little girl who was very naughty."

Out of the blue, she takes my right hand, yanks it onto her lap, and presses it flat on the cover of the book.

"Our provisional operating table for today," she announces with a chuckle.

I clench my teeth. The pain has returned in full. As has my fear. Then Mother takes the pencil and presses it down firmly on my swollen finger.

I scream. Stars dance around my room.

"Keep still," she hisses, wrapping the bandage around my finger. "What's wrong with you children? You've both been behaving so oddly these past few days." She pulls the bandage tighter. "Is there any reason for it?"

I say nothing.

"Your father was badly injured by the strangers," she says, taking a deep breath. "Father almost died from a stab wound that became critically inflamed. And you know full well that we can't go to see a doctor for help. Is this how you show your gratitude? By lying and being disobedient?"

Please, dear God, make her stop this, I plead, staring at my bandaged hand. With each further layer, the pain gets worse, creeping up my arm to my shoulder blade.

"I'm only going to ask you once." She pauses briefly, putting the bandage to one side. "I don't want to hear any of your cock-and-bull stories, Juno. Understood?" Resting her hand on my shoulder, she strokes my skin, then digs her fingertips into my neck. "Did you go secretly into Father's library? Into his study?"

My forefinger begins to tingle beneath the bandage. Blood is surging into every limb like a raging river, pumping up my finger like a wheelbarrow tire.

The pain is becoming unbearable.

"No, Mother," I say through gritted teeth.

"Where were you, then?"

"In the shed."

Mother gives me a searching look, then nods. A crooked smile forms on her lips. I can't tell if she believes me. Tying the ends of the bandage into a tight knot, she pushes my hand off the book. "All done."

The bandaging around my hand reminds me of a snowball. I feel chilled to the bone as if it were deepest winter, even though the sun is streaming into my bedroom.

"You're a grown woman now, Juno," Mother says, shifting closer to me. "I can remember what that feels like. In the springtime of life, when the buds are about to open." She smiles. "I was fifteen once, you know. But that's over forty years ago." Leaning over to the bedside table, Mother reaches for the jug of ice cubes. "Each time my period came, the urge for freedom and independence got greater." She shakes the ice in the glass; it's started to melt. "It's perfectly normal. But unlike you, I was interested in quite different things at your age, like maths, biology, and boys." Mother holds the jug up to my nose. "So tell me, Juno. Why fairy tales? What does a young woman like you find so fascinating about children's stories when you'd rather read *Juliette*? All this wanting to read Boy a story is just a pretense." She moves so close to me that I can smell her breath, a spicy mixture of fresh mint, porridge, and smoked herring. "Did you perhaps hide something in this book? Something secret, perhaps, something you don't want me to see?"

I can barely breathe.

"No, Mother. Nothing."

She takes my bandaged hand and plunges it into the molten iced water. A moment later, I can feel the wet bandage like a second skin around my fingers, which instinctively want to clench into a fist, but the pencil stops them. Then the iced water starts to burn like a thousand bee stings. A symphony of pain. In agitation I try to pull my hand out of the jug, but Mother's iron grip keeps it in place. "Well, if that's the case, you won't mind me checking the book, will you?"

I grit my teeth and shake my head. I've no idea what Mother's getting at.

She holds my fingers for a few more seconds in the iced water, then finally lets go. I yank my hand out of the jug and wrap the duvet around the soaked bandage. The stinging pain subsides at once.

Mother has opened the book and is examining every page, running her fingertips across the paper. What does she imagine she's going to find?

Holding it close to her face, she keeps searching. "You know, I was badly hurt once, too, Juno. Seriously ill. Worse than a broken finger." She turns the cover of the book in her hands, inspecting it from every angle. "A broken heart. Do you understand? You can't make that better so easily with a pencil..."

Mother breaks off mid-sentence. She freezes like a person in a photograph.

The tips of her fingers are feeling the inside of the cover. She turns to me and glares. "Liar! I knew it!"

Baffled, I stare at her fingers.

She begins to pick away at the corner of the protective paper, then rips it off in one go, leaving a few scraps hanging from the cardboard.

I swallow.

To my astonishment a carefully folded piece of pink paper appears, which must have been hidden beneath. Why haven't I noticed it all these years?

"What's that?" Mother asks sternly, unfolding the paper. I shrug nervously.

Her eyes grow large.

Silence.

She scrunches up the pink piece of paper, stuffs it into the pocket of her apron and gets to her feet. “You're going to stay in your room all day!”

“But I haven't done anything,” I plead as she opens the door to my room.

“Was that a message?” I add, my thoughts spinning around my head. I'm convinced it must be a secret message to me. Pink paper. Written and hidden by my big sister.

“Please, Mother!” I cry. “Who's the message from?”

Without a word she steps out onto the landing, slamming the door behind her.

I sit on my bed, staring at the *cellulare* in my hand. It's been half an hour since Mother left my room. I expect she's keeping an eye on my brother. I'm really worried about Boy's health. He urgently needs a doctor; he hit his head hard.

But for that we'd have to get off the island, and we can't if Luca doesn't come and rescue us soon. I tap the circular picture on the glass and put the device to my ear. A strange beeping, as rhythmical as the throbbing pain in my finger. Then a crackle, and Luca's distant voice sounding very close, as if he were sitting beside me on the bed, his head with its tousled hair leaning on my shoulder.

“Elly?” His voice is quivering.

“Yes,” I whisper.

“I heard everything.” He sounds tense. “Are you OK? Please say something, Elly!”

“Don't worry about me,” I reply, looking at my bandaged hand. My broken finger burns like fire beneath the cold, wet bandage. “I sorted it all out. But my brother is in urgent need of help. I think Boy has a concussion. That's what Mother said, at least. When can you come and get us, Luca? We need to get away from here!"

"Listen, Elly, I explained everything to my *capo* a few minutes ago." He hesitates. "The team needed to be told how serious the situation is. With you and Boy. So I told him about us. I told him I'd seen you twice on the island."

"Did you get into trouble?" I ask, worried for him. But Luca doesn't reply. I can only hear his breathing, heavy and irregular. I wonder how badly he was punished. When he still doesn't reply, I whisper, "Luca, what did they do to you?"

"They're coming to get you. Today. You're going to be saved!"

Relief immediately floods my uptight body. I feel a tingling all over, and even the pain in my tense shoulders fades. The healing power of hope is beginning to take effect. "When?" I burst into tears. "Luca, when are they coming to the island?"

"The team is getting everything ready for the rescue operation," Luca whispers. "But they have to wait for nightfall, Elly. The landing is planned for eleven o'clock."

I glance at the alarm clock on my bedside table.

Almost seven more hours.

"I don't know if Boy's going to be better by then."

Silence. I hear Luca's breathing again, shallow and ponderous. Then he calls out something into the room. A brief pause then another man says something in a language I don't understand. He's probably talking to his *capo*. Their conversation gets louder. Luca sounds furious.

I squint at the bedroom door.

"They'll be coming with divers and boats. Can you carry your brother to the shore?"

I think of the medieval show we put on for Mother and Father in the garden last year. I was the horse and Boy the knight in armor on my back. On that occasion I didn't find it hard to haul my eleven-year-old brother down to the tool shed. Over the winter, however, Boy has shot up like a vine.

"I'll try," I say, even though I don't know how I'll be able to get Boy out of his room unnoticed. With a broken finger and wary mother.

"*Bene*, good," Luca says. He doesn't sound particularly confident. "Tonight at eleven o'clock, then. At our secret meeting place by the shore. Everything is going to be fine, Elly. And please be careful!"

I notice again the book of fairy tales on the bedside table. The scraps of paper ripped from the gray cardboard. I think of the pink note safely hidden in there for years. "I had a sister, too," I say softly. "She died many years ago. Drowned in the lake."

"What?" Luca sounds alarmed.

"Her name was Ruth," I reply, recalling the newspaper cutting, the bright-yellow tracksuit top. "She was abducted from a campsite when she was six, somewhere in the mountains. Switzerland, I think."

"How do you know?"

"I snuck into Father's library and found an old photo album," I say hesitantly. "It's got square photos and newspaper cuttings stuck in."

"*Brava*, Elly," Luca says. "You did really well. I will pass on the information about Ruth to my colleagues right now. Can you bring the photo album tonight? It's important evidence."

"I hid it in the shed."

"In a safe place?"

"I think so," I say, though all of a sudden I'm not so sure. "It's possible my brother saw me putting it into the fishing box," I say thoughtfully. "But Boy definitely won't say anything."

"Elly, we can't risk him telling your mother. Do you understand? Your life is in danger if they find out you know about the kidnappings. You need to get the album out of the shed as quickly as possible!"

I think about this for a moment.

There's a real danger that Mother would catch me doing it. But Luca's right. We'll be in just as much trouble if Boy blurts out the secret, maybe in his delirium, especially as I know he talks in his sleep. Like me. And Mother's keeping watch beside his bed. I have no other choice.

"I'll try."

"Thanks, Elly," he whispers. His voice is soft and warm, at once hopeful and concerned. "*Stammi bene*. Trust me, Elly, tonight you'll be free."

I want to tell him how much I miss him, how often I find myself thinking about him, but Luca has already gone.

Disappointed, I put the little black case in my lap and look at my closed bedroom door. No footsteps on the landing, not a sound in the house. I push the thing back under my mattress, get off the bed, go over to the window, and open it as wide as I can.

Fresh air comes rushing into my nose.

I look down at our vegetable patch, then my eyes drift over to the old well, past the two birch trees, to Ruth's grave, then the tall loudspeaker masts, finally coming to a stop at the red tool shed.

Dangerous. But I can do it.

Dark storm clouds are gathering on the horizon.

20

I open my wardrobe and take out the scratchy, gray winter jumper. Not because I'm cold. On the contrary, I'm sweating from every pore. My forehead and back are dripping. But I need somewhere to hide the album in case I'm caught on my way back. It's a baggy jumper, and there's plenty of space for the slim book. Going out onto the landing, I close the door behind me. On the way I stop outside Boy's door and listen. But it's silent: no snoring, no voices, not even Mother's. Relieved, I run my bandaged hand over the wooden veneer. So long as Boy's asleep, he can't reveal the hiding place. Which gives me a bit of time. Mother will be keeping watch at his bedside while I sort out a new place to hide the album, somewhere safer, maybe in the bathroom or storeroom, until the danger has passed.

Only seven hours to go, Boy.

Till we're rescued.

Hang in there!

We've almost made it.

The stairs creak as I shuffle my way down. I hold on to the

banister more tightly, putting all my weight onto my right hand, gritting my teeth. Finally I'm in the hall. Now I just have to go through the kitchen door into the vegetable garden and then—I go rigid.

Mother.

She's stirring a pot at the cooker. The sweet aroma of elderflower, cherry, and wild strawberries is wafting from the kitchen. She turns around to me.

"Why aren't you in your room?" The surprise in her voice is unmistakable. And I feel paralyzed.

"I..." I stutter, unable to think of an answer. I instinctively clasp my hands behind my back.

"May I remind you that you're not allowed out of your room?"

"Yes, Mother."

"So?"

"I just wanted to get a glass of milk."

"In a woolly jumper?"

"I felt cold," I say, then point at the steaming pot to change the subject. "Are you making fruit purée? Smells wonderful."

Mother shakes her head.

"Is Boy alone in his room? I thought you were keeping watch beside his bed."

"Father's taken over," she replies as she keeps stirring. "I've got something important to do." Taking the spoon out of the pot, Mother checks the amber liquid that oozes thickly down the wooden handle. "I'm making jelly."

I wander over to the cooker. I love this smell. Immediately I think of our safe room, which I've associated with the irresistible tang of fruit since I was a child.

Mother puts the pot on a massive wooden board and slides the rusty metal cover over the hob. Then she picks up a dark-gray granite bowl from the work surface in front of her and holds it up to my nose. I peer in.

Big white pills.

Comfort pills.

"But we've still got a full tube of them, haven't we?" I ask, confused. "In the safe room," I add, pointing with my bandaged hand at the cellar hatch hidden by the rug.

"Those were placebos, my girl," she replies, dipping a teaspoon into the orange mass. I don't know what she's talking about. Mother stares at me, then smiles sympathetically because she can read the expression on my face.

"Placebos have no pharmacological effect," she explains, pulling the sticky teaspoon out of the pot, blowing on the jelly, and tasting it. "But don't worry, Juno. After today, your comfort pills will actually make you better. They're nice and strong."

Reaching into the front pocket of her checked apron, she takes out a half-empty tube of pills and shakes it like a bell. "This is the real medicine for you children," she says, placing the unopened tube beside the huge stone bowl. "The time has come, you see, to prepare ourselves for an emergency."

"What effect do they have?" I ask, as I don't understand the significance of the new pills.

"You silly billy," Mother says, rolling her eyes at me. "All those times in the safe room over the years were just drills. I thought you'd understood that. The new pills will help you become really calm. They combat nerves and fear. Fear of the strangers." She dips the spoon into the jelly and hands it to me. "Does it need more sugar?"

I take the spoon and gaze at the runny amber jelly. It's still steaming, so I give it a blow. Why's Mother suddenly being so friendly? She's never let me taste her special jelly before; it's been for drills only. I lick the spoon.

At once the delicious flavor spreads across my tongue and gums. A grin forms on my lips. The fruity mass is warm and as sweet as honey. I nod. "Excellent, Mother. Better than the old ones."

"That's what I thought," she says, giving a satisfied smile. Taking a pestle, she grinds a few pills in the granite mortar until it looks like fresh powder snow. Then she tips the powder into the steaming pot, stirring it into the jelly. "We're going to put some of the medicine into the fruity coating. As a precaution. But don't worry, I've added more sugar to make it nicer."

Why nicer? I'm confused. We like the comfort pills as they are, Mother knows that. I get the uncanny feeling that something's not right. Why is it so important to her that we take them?

"The new comfort pills also give pain relief," Mother says, smiling and nodding at my bandaged hand. "But only in an emergency. We still hope the break will heal by itself, don't we?"

"Are we having another practice soon, then?" I ask in astonishment, looking out of the kitchen window. A small, blue bird is sitting on the loudspeaker mast, preening its feathers.

"We've done enough practices, Juno," Mother replies, opening the cutlery drawer. "The danger is all around. The strangers have found out where we live. They could come onto the island at any moment and take you away."

If only she knew how right she was.

I look at the ticking clock above the sink. A red plastic cat whose eyes and crooked tail swing back and forth, marking the seconds.

We loved it when we were children. But right now I hate it.

Because it's showing me the time. Only ten minutes have passed, ten agonizingly long minutes. The hours until Luca comes to fetch us don't seem to be passing. Before that I've got to sneak down to the tool shed and get the photo album without arousing Mother and Father's suspicion. But how? Mother's going to be here in the kitchen a while longer, preparing the new comfort pills.

"When do you think Boy will be able to get up again?" I ask as casually as possible, as Mother takes two tablet molds from the top cupboard and places them neatly beside the pot.

"Your brother is making good progress," she replies, putting on an oven glove. "He was lucky. Just a bump, but no concussion."

"Does that mean he can walk again?" I ask. My hope is growing that I won't have to carry him down to the shore tonight.

"Well, I expect he'll have to spend another forty-eight hours in bed," Mother says, pouring the jelly into the small individual molds. "As a precaution."

Two days. Shit.

Mother opens the half-full tube of pills and shakes the rest onto the work surface. Like flower chafers, they jump in all directions, as if trying to get away from her. She takes a pair of tweezers and puts each one of the white pills into the forms full of hot jelly. She looks concentrated. The orange-yellow jelly spills over the edge of the mold like molten lava. The amber coating of the comfort pills is ready.

"Can I just pop into the garden?" I ask tentatively.

"No, you're confined to your room."

"I just want to pick a few flowers for Boy."

"Your brother needs peace and quiet, not flowers."

"Please, Mother," I beg her.

"Oh, bloody hell!" she curses, dropping the tweezers as if they were red hot. She rubs her eyelids. Steam must have gotten into her eyes. She scuttles to the sink, turns on the tap and splashes water on her face. Then she pauses, grabs the dishcloth, and pats her face. Turning to me angrily, she snarls, "How often have I told you not to interrupt me while I'm cooking?"

"I'm sorry," I whisper, staring at a drop of water on her cheek. It looks like a teardrop. This unusual image seems strangely familiar, as if it had etched itself somewhere deep in my memory. I can't help thinking of our bunker again.

Of the hole, the strangers, the false alarm.

It was last Sunday when I saw Mother cry for the third time in my life. During our drill. A rare event, because Mother is big on etiquette. Always keen that we don't see her when she's sad or having one of her melancholy days. This is why I remember the other two times she was in tears. Many years ago, down by the big rock when Boy ate the strange berries.

When he was on the verge of death.

Mother cried then.

And when Ruth drowned.

But why on Sunday when she gave us the comfort pills? In the bunker during a harmless practice? I mean, nobody's life was in danger.

The realization hits me with full force, like a blow to the stomach. My tummy clenches. I have to lean forward, and I feel sick. My thoughts are reeling, and the voice inside my head keeps screaming at me:

Mother is going to poison us! She's going to poison us!

That's why Mother was crying in the safe room. Because at that moment she thought about losing us for real.

I can taste bile in my mouth.

Oh, God, she's preparing poison pills!

Looking over at me, Mother's eyes open wide and she drops the pot. Rushing over, she grabs my shoulders and shakes me. "Are you alright? What's wrong?"

"Leave me alone!" I groan.

"Did you swallow some of the powder?" she screams at me in a panic. Her voice is shrill and overwrought. She shakes me again. "Answer me, Juno! Tell me!"

"No."

"Are you sure?"

"Yes," I reply, swallowing the acrid bile back down. I have to pull myself together. I can't give her any cause for suspicion, mustn't show any fear. I slowly sit back up, smooth my dress, and try to look her in the eye. "I'm better now. Don't worry." I wipe my brow with the scratchy sleeve. She mustn't realize that I've guessed the deadly truth about her pills, the reason why she's made them. Even though I can't understand Mother. Why does she want to kill us? "I think I'm getting my period."

Mother turns abruptly to our calendar that hangs beside the fridge. "But you shouldn't be starting for another four days."

"But that's what it feels like, Mother," I shoot back at her, feeling my finger beneath the bandage. Luckily Mother can't tell when I'm lying anymore. The pain has been worth it; finally my thoughts are free.

"Yes, it's possible" Mother says, coming toward me. "I remember it wasn't always regular." She looks at me as if I were a stranger. "And you're absolutely sure you didn't take any of my medicine, the white powder?"

I feel such a shiver run down my spine that I shudder involuntarily. This is the proof. Mother has just given me confirmation. Her pills are poison.

"I only licked the spoon," I reply, pointing at the pot behind her. "Just the jelly. Like you."

She thinks about it and nods. Relief in her face.

"I feel tired, Mother," I say feebly. And this isn't a lie. "Can I go up to bed?"

"Do that," Mother says, turning back to the cooker and picking up a spoon. "And tell your father that I'll take over from him as soon as I'm done down here."

"Of course, Mother." I say, hurrying to the kitchen door. I steal a glance into the garden, glimpsing the rotten wooden cross on Ruth's grave. Black rain clouds over the woods. I'm certain a storm will break out soon.

I stop in the doorway and turn to Mother, who's pouring the rest of the fruit jelly into the tablet molds. I wait until she's finished her highly concentrated work and then ask, my eyes still fixed on the front pocket of her apron where she put the secret message, "Mother, what was on that pink piece of paper? Was it a message for me? You've got to tell me, please! Is it a message from my sister?"

She gives me a searching look, slaps her skirt, and shakes her head. "Your big sister is dead, and she ought to remain that way."

I don't understand what she means. My curiosity makes me feel twitchy; I can't leave it at that, so I try again. "When did she write the message? Can't you tell me that, at least? Please, Mother!"

She puts the pot back down onto the cooker. A sweet gust of cherry aroma meets my nose. Mother actually seems to be considering if she should answer my question.

"Shortly before her accident," she says faintly. It's barely audible. Then she whips around and stands up straight to her full height. "Believe me, Juno. You mustn't read the message. It's for your own safety. Now go!" she says, pointing to the door.

"Thanks, Mother," I say, curtseying before dashing out into the hall. The feeling of relief, certainty, gives me renewed courage. Even though I don't have a new plan of how to fetch the photo album from the tool shed.

My feet carry me up the stairs; I have to be careful not to stumble. The hidden message in my book of fairy tales *was* from my sister. Mother just confirmed it.

A secret message from Ruth to me.

But what did she write?

21

There's talking coming from Boy's room. I can hear Father. His deep voice comes booming out onto the landing. He seems to be speaking to someone.

Oh, no! I realize at once what that means. I hurry to the open door; my brother must be awake.

I enter the small room. The curtains are drawn. It's stuffy and smells of body odor. Boy's sitting on his bed, cross-legged. Beside him Father's in a chair, his arms crossed.

Boy smiles when he sees me.

"What are you doing here?" Father snaps. "You're supposed to be confined to your room. Have you forgotten?"

"I just wanted to check on Boy. See whether he was still in pain." I curtsey to show humility; it usually works. "Can I come in?"

Father mutters something unintelligible and nods.

"How are you feeling?" I ask, sitting on the mattress. I put my hand on his duvet, causing a puff of fusty air to escape from underneath.

"Better," he says. Color has returned to his face.

"Wasn't so bad, just a bump," Father says, patting Boy's head. He winces.

"Be careful, Father!" I plead.

"Oh come on; it's not that bad," he replies coldly, leaning on the bedpost. "Could you take over for a bit, Juno? I urgently need the loo."

"Of course, Father."

Father gets up from the chair and wobbles toward the door. He still seems drunk. Or has he been drinking again?

I wait until he's left the room, then I get up briskly from the bed. Following Father onto the landing, I wait impatiently until I hear the key in the bathroom has been turned twice. Then I return to Boy's room, shut the door, and sit down on his mattress again. My pulse is racing.

"What's up?" Boy says. I can't hide anything from my brother; he knows me too well.

"Did he ask you about the tool shed?"

Boy gives a faint shake of the head and grimaces.

"Thank God."

"Juno, what did you hide there?" he asks, shifting closer to me. "Mother wouldn't make such a fuss over a silly romance, would she?"

I take a very deep breath. My head says I should lie to him, but my gut feeling is the opposite. I glance nervously at the door. In seven hours we'll be leaving this island at last, but I'm going to need Boy's help. He'll only follow me if he knows the truth. I look at him seriously and whisper, "Mother and Father aren't our parents."

"What?" Boy puts his head on his shoulder and laughs.

"I'm serious, Boy," I say as quietly as possible, but my voice is quivering. Boy notices. His smile vanishes. So I continue quickly. "I've got proof. An old photo album in Father's library."

"What sort of proof?"

"We were kidnapped," I whisper. "You and me. And Ruth, our big sister."

Boy looks at me in disbelief.

"My name is Elly," I say with a thumping in my chest. "Elly Watson. I'm from England originally. Father and Mother lured me away from the beach in Southland—its real name is in fact Italy—when I was two. And then secretly brought me to the island here."

"Who says so?"

"Luca," I say curtly, my mouth as dry as a handful of flour. "And Mother's photo album is proof."

"Luca?" My brother frowns. "Who's Luca?"

"A guard with the Italian police," I reply. "They've been looking for us all over the world for years. Luca showed me a newspaper cutting, a missing person announcement. It had a photo of me as a child and next to it one of what I might look like now. Uncle Ole recognized me at the window and notified the guards." I pause; the truth sounds even more unbelievable when you say it out loud. "But Father must have found out and followed Uncle Ole to the other side of the lake." I swallow. "And then he killed him."

Boy's mouth is wide open.

"That's why Father came back covered in blood that night, do you understand? It wasn't his own blood."

"Father killed Uncle Ole?"

"Yes."

"And what about me? Was I also..." He hesitates.

I bow my head and stroke the bandage on my right hand. My finger hurts.

"I don't understand any of this, Juno," Boy says, rubbing his cheek. It's glowing bright red. "Why would Mother and Father kidnap you? It doesn't make any sense."

"I don't think Mother can have children anymore. In another album in Father's study I found a picture of Mother with a big belly. But no baby. At least there weren't any photos of a child. The pages were empty. Maybe she lost it; there seems to be a curse over her family. Like in *Thumbelina*. And that's why we were brought here to the island. As replacements."

"I think you've been reading too many fairy stories, Juno," he says, looking at me incredulously. "And what's this Luca guy got to do with it?"

"He's going to save both of us!" I reply. "Tonight!"

Boy drops back onto the pillow and shakes his head. He stares stiffly at the other side of the room, taking shallow breaths as his forehead is furrowed by ever deeper lines.

I'd love to be able to give my brother more time to digest the truth, but it's time we don't have. Father will be back any moment, and before then, I've got to spell out just how bad it would be if someone found the hidden photo album in the shed. Besides, we need to work out how we can get to the shore undetected tonight.

"Can you walk down to the lake?" I ask. "Do you think you could do that on your own?"

Boy turns to me. The color has drained from his face. He gives me a serious look. "You don't really believe all of that stuff, do you?"

"What do you mean?"

"That story. That we were kidnapped and that Father's a killer. What are you playing at?"

I look at him in surprise. Maybe I've blurted it all out too quickly.

Too much new information, too many improbable things. I can understand my little brother. "Listen to me, Boy," I say emphatically, because the time for longer explanations is slipping away. "I'm not lying. It's the truth!"

Boy's eyes instinctively dart to my bandaged hand and narrows his eyes. "How are you going to prove it? Without that funny thing around your finger I'd at least be able to tell if you were ly–"

"Do you want me to undo the bandage?" I say, interrupting him more angrily than I'd intended. I hold out my fingers. "I'm telling the truth."

Boy appears to ponder this.

For the first time in my life, my stupid bloody forefinger could be helpful, but I've broken it. I bite my lower lip. What can I do to make my brother believe me? All these years it's been normal for him to take my twitching as a sign I'm lying. But that won't work anymore. Annoyed, I let my hand fall into my lap. I can't see any other option than to take off the bandage. Maybe I'll still be able to move my finger. Even if it causes me unimaginable pain.

Boy watches me expectantly.

Alright, then. Both our lives are at stake here; I don't have a choice. I'm just about to undo the knot around my wrist when the door springs open.

Father appears, clutching the handle. "You can go back to your room now, Juno," he croaks.

I give a start. How come he's back so quickly?

"What are you waiting for? Go!" Father's getting impatient.

I nervously lean forward to Boy and whisper in his ear, "Not a word about the shed! Or they'll kill us!"

"Now!" Father barks, waving toward the landing.

I gently brush my brother's forehead with the fingers of my left hand and leave the room without saying anything.

Please, Boy, don't tell on me.

I lie on the bed and close my tired eyes. Just a little rest. Time to collect my thoughts. I'm not used to so much upheaval. Apart from Uncle Ole's visits, our life on the island offers little by way of change, or much cause for concern because we've gotten used to the anxiety. Heightened vigilance is part and parcel of our daily existence.

But the past few days have been different, new, draining. Ever since I discovered that the strangers don't live on the other side of the lake but just one room down the hall.

Pulling the duvet over my head, I hide in my soft den. It immediately gets darker and warmer, and I feel safe, protected. I lack the energy to contemplate whether it was a mistake to tell Boy about Mother's photo album.

Through the duvet I can hear the muffled, metallic ticking of the alarm clock. What's the time, actually? I'm too exhausted to look. I'm just going to lie here for ten minutes.

I focus on every stroke.

Tick, tock. Tick, tock.

It's soothing. I begin to breathe more slowly. Maybe I could at least grab half an hour's nap before going to fetch the photo album from the shed. I need to recharge my batteries. For tonight, when Luca comes with the police. For our secret flight from the island. My eyelids grow heavier. I feel the weight of my body on the mattress.

My mind pictures Luca, his black hair, his sweet, turned-up nose, his lips. Oh Luca, we'll see each other again soon.

I can't help yawning.

Then I nod off.

PART THREE

22

I wrench my eyes open. A rasping sound has woken me from my dreamless sleep. I fling the duvet off me and feel the itchy wool jumper sticking to my skin. My forehead is covered in a film of sweat. How long was I asleep? Anxiously I roll over to face the bedside table; the alarm clock says 9:56.

About an hour to go. Breathing a sigh of relief, I take off the jumper, drop back down onto the bed, and stare at the ceiling. It's dark. The tangy scent of twinflowers and pine needles hangs in my room. But there's another unfamiliar smell, faintly smoky and spicy. Like when Father burns the autumn leaves. Thank God I didn't oversleep. I can't bear to contemplate what would have happened if I hadn't turned up at the shore on time. How could I fall asleep?

The distant call of a Ural owl, as clear as if the bird were sitting on the edge of my bed. Strange, I think, as a sudden gust of cold air catches my bare legs. I feel chilly. Did I leave the window open? Mystified, I turn over to the other side of the bed, and stiffen.

She's standing silently by the open window, her arms crossed over her chest, and in her right hand glows a little white stick. Bringing it up to her mouth, Mother purses her lips and sucks in. Her cheeks sink to the bones, then she blows little white clouds out of her nose and mouth. The smoky smell wafts over to me.

"I'd actually stopped," she says. "But because of you I fished out this old packet."

I don't understand.

She sucks on the stick again; her fingers are trembling. It takes a few seconds before the clouds of smoke come streaming out of her mouth again. "Why did you lie to me, Juno?"

My palms are turning wet. Not knowing what to say to her, I shrug.

"You went into Father's library without permission."

I vigorously shake my head.

"Yes, you did, my girl. I have proof," she says calmly. The stick dangles from her lips. "Don't take me for a fool, Juno. I checked, you see? The window in the study? You didn't think of that. It wasn't properly closed. You had to climb into the garden because I'd locked the door, thank goodness. I'd never have noticed otherwise."

Light-gray plumes of smoke come streaming from her nostrils. Mother looks like an angry bull about to launch an attack. "So tell me, Juno. What were you looking for?"

My heart sinks. Mother knows. The open window. Of course I couldn't shut it properly from outside. How could I have forgotten that? I rack my brains for an answer. It has to sound convincing enough for Mother to believe me. My forefinger pulses beneath the bandage.

Juliette, or The Love of My Life—the only answer that Mother might think is the truth. I hope. Sitting up in bed, I place my hands in my lap and play the guilty girl. "I'm sorry, Mother. Yes, you're right. I was in Father's study. I crept in there to secretly read your novel.

About Juliette and Richard Blackwood. I don't know why, but stories about love have started to interest me recently," I say softly—and it's no lie. I put on a girly smile. "Please don't punish me, Mother. Don't you think it's nice that we like the same stories?"

"Cock-and-bull stories?" she says, deadly serious.

"What?"

Mother stares at me. I can't read the expression on her face. She sucks silently on her little stick once more as she looks at me contemptuously. Then she turns her back to me, leans against the window frame and peers down into the garden. Is she looking at our shed?

Her shiny, greasy hair is tied into a bun. Like a glazed cinnamon roll, I think, wondering when she last washed it. In anticipation of an answer, I lean forward. "Mother? Are you really angry at me for having read your novel even though I'm not allowed to? It's just a silly book."

I can see her hands shaking. Suddenly she spins around to face me. Her face is as red as a beetroot. Her whole body is simmering like water on the boil.

"Where's my *Book of Consolation*?" she says, spitting each word out individually.

I swallow.

Mother sucks nervously on her stick, then again and again, without letting me out of her sight. Her body is enveloped in a fog. "My album? For God's sake, tell me where you've hidden it! It's not on the bookshelf!"

"I don't know what you're talking about," I stammer.

Mother gives a throaty laugh and shakes her head. "You know, Juno, your big sister was as inquisitive as you. In this respect, the two of you are very much alike. Her name was Ruth, but I bet you know that now." She glares at me. "Ruth often swam to the other side, even though we'd expressly forbidden it. But she refused to listen. She kept saying, *Happiness lives on the other side of the lake. We deserve this happiness, too.*" Mother laughs again. "Quite the poet, wasn't she?"

I can't help thinking of the lucky stone that my sister gave me. It's from the other side, she explained proudly as she put the shiny black stone in my hand. I used to find that fanciful—a magic object from the other shore—I was convinced she'd made it up. But the notion that her story corresponded to the truth allowed me to dream of it, for a time at least.

So it's true. Ruth *did* swim all that way to the other shore.

"It was inexcusable. Father and I made a really big mistake," Mother says, taking another suck of her stick. "Your sister was just too old when we got her from the Swiss mountains. Not as gullible as you and boy. Ruth wasn't a little girl anymore—we never considered that."

Why's Mother suddenly telling me the truth? I feel hot all over. What's she got in store?

"That's why Father had to punish Ruth. Do you understand? To protect us. To protect you, Juno. It wasn't easy. She was our first child. But sooner or later, your sister would have told the police about us. Ruth was a bright girl. She understood everything. She knew we weren't her real parents. And besides, she was with us on our Italian holiday when we picked you out on the beach in Riccione."

Picked out? I feel sick.

"And because we didn't want to lose any more children after the tragic death of your sister, we forbade you and Boy from learning how to swim. To minimize the risk that you might escape. Surely you understand that, don't you?"

A single shoe on the shore. Black storm clouds in the sky, Mother on her knees. Screaming on the damp ground, her hands over her eyes. The blue-checkered wool blanket that Father lays over Ruth's lifeless body.

My stomach is knotting. In my mind, the images from that dramatic night flare up once more. Ruth still had one shoe on, a red sandal, on her left foot. My favorite shoe that I wear every day, the one with the silver round buckle.

I taste bile in my mouth, tart and bitter. No, no: Ruth wasn't swimming in the lake; she still had her shoes on.

It wasn't an accident.

Father drowned Ruth by the shore.

"Get up, Juno, and come to the window," Mother says softly, a crooked grin on her lips. "I'd like to show you something."

I don't move a muscle. I can't. My body seems to be shackled to the bed. An invisible weight is pushing me ever deeper into the mattress. Mother is jiggling her foot, waiting for a reaction.

Please, dear God, let this just be a bad dream, I pray when Mother's smile vanishes. She lunges forward, grabs my bandaged hand, and drags me to the window. I scream as my forearm is convulsed by a sharp pain; this is no dream. With all her strength Mother pushes me up to the window and snarls in my ear, "Look out there, traitor! We haven't got forever!"

Our vegetable patch. Ruth's grave. A few meters further is the tool shed, and beyond that the dark lake. The moon is setting in the sky.

"Recognize that?" she murmurs from behind. I feel her hot breath on my cheek. A revolting smell of stale smoke and dried fish assaults my nose.

What does she mean? Desperately I squint and stare into the

darkness. Mother pushes me harder against the windowsill. As the narrow wooden ledge digs into my stomach I retch again.

"There! Look!" she snaps. "There, on the water!"

Finally I see it, behind the silhouette of a tall birch tree, in the middle of the lake. A boat rocking on the shining water. A little rowing boat!

I'm seized by panic. Is that Luca?

Wresting myself free from Mother, I turn to the bedside table with my clock. I need to know what time it is. But I can't see the hands from here.

Is Luca too early?

Mother grasps my throat and pushes me back to the window. A hiss and a burning sensation on my cheek. Her white stick has touched my skin. I scream.

"Tell me what you see!"

I stare down at the lake again, rubbing my cheek. Maybe Luca will be able to see me up here at the window if I wave with both arms and scream.

The pain has gone from my cheek. Or I've blocked it out, in excitement and hope. Think, Juno. It may be a few hundred meters to Luca's boat, but there's a clear view. Yes, it's a possibility. Eventually I recognize his outline from this distance, his hooded jumper, his hat.

I falter.

Wait. That isn't headgear. Or is it? I lean further out of the window. The cold night air caresses my face. Who is that? Now my eyes are no more than two narrow slits. I hold my breath. That isn't Luca on the boat. How could I have gotten that wrong? It's the blurred silhouettes of two people. What I took to be a hat was just another head. There are two people on the boat. A big one and a little one.

"What does this mean?" The words come blurting out of my mouth.

"It's very simple, Juno," Mother says calmly, as if she were explaining a recipe. She sucks the rest of her glowing stick. "If you don't tell me immediately where you've hidden my *Book of Consolation*, Father will act in response. Understood? When I give the agreed upon sign, he'll throw him overboard." She coughs, squashes what's left of her stick on my window frame, and flicks it into the garden. I watch the sparks rain down onto our vegetable patch. "He'll push Boy into the water, do you understand?"

I feel paralyzed.

"Well, then. Where is it?"

"He...he can't swim," I say, still utterly numb.

"I'm going to count to ten, Juno," Mother says, reaching into her apron and taking out a lighter and a small cardboard box, from which she plucks another of her little white sticks. "If you haven't given me the answer by then, you'll be an only child again. Do you understand, Juno?" She flicks the lighter once, twice, and I instantly recognize the grating sound that woke me up. Greedily she holds the stick to the flame and sucks. Then she blows her stinking smoke into my face. "One."

"Mother, please don't!"

"Two."

"It's not Boy's fault!"

"Three."

"I really don't know where your album–"

"Four."

"Don't do this! Please! Make Father bring him back!"

"Boy is going to die. He'll die a miserable death. Seven!"

"Stop it! I beg you!"

"Nine."

"In the shed!" I scream, my voice now shrill. "In the shed, Mother. I hid your album in the shed. In the fishing box!"

"Why didn't you tell me earlier?" Mother says coolly. She takes another, long suck on the stick and holds the smoke in her mouth for ages. Then she gives a nod of satisfaction and tosses the burning stick out of the window. "OK, Juno. Let's go."

"But what about Boy?" I beg, pointing anxiously at the lake.

Mother seems to think about this for a second, then waves at Father with both arms over her head. I look down at the rocking boat in apprehension. The two silhouettes move. The larger of the two returns Mother's gesture, sticking both arms up. Then Mother pushes me away from the window and drags me behind her like a whiny child. She has an iron grip on my arm.

That's it.

I'm never going to see Luca again.

Tears roll down my cheeks. Juno, what are you going to do now? If Mother gets her hands on the photo album, then it's all over. They'll kill us. Like they did Ruth. The voices inside my head get louder. You mustn't give up! Are you listening? You are Elly. Elly from England. You don't belong on this island! Fight, Elly, fight!

When we're out on the landing, I tear myself away from Mother and run back into my room.

"What the hell are you doing?" Mother growls. Her head appears in the doorway. I can hear the bafflement in her voice.

"Jumper!" I call out over my shoulder. "Just my jumper, Mother. It's cold outside!"

We hurry down the stairs, across the hall, through the kitchen and into the garden. Thick storm clouds hang over the lake, and it's turned much chillier. Taking big strides, Mother stumbles through our vegetable patch while I keep my eyes fixed on the water. Then I finally see him: Father, rowing back to the shore with labored strokes. With Boy. He's alive! I exhale, relieved.

"You'd better not have lied to me again, Juno," Mother gasps, dragging me past the well, Ruth's grave, making a beeline for the tool shed. She's panting as she opens the door to the shed. Fine sand trickles down on us. We stop in the middle of the shed, both of us out of breath. Mother's eyes dart around, frantically searching. "Where is the fishing box?" she coughs.

"Over there!" I say quietly, moving toward the shelves.

"What are you waiting for? Take it out!"

I grab the heavy metal box, put it on the floor and open the metal clasp. Mother stands behind me; I can feel her breath on my neck. I flip open the lid.

"You filthy liar!" Mother spits.

I shudder.

The photo album has disappeared.

"I...I don't understand, Mother, it *was* here," I stammer. Mother yanks me up by my hair, shakes me and screams at me as if she's gone mad. "You're going to pay for this, Juno!"

She violently hauls me out of the shed, throws me on the wet ground and stands over me. "As punishment you're going to spend five days in the cellar!"

"Please, not the safe room," I plead.

Then she hits me in the face.

23

From the corner of my eye I can see Father take the rifle off the stone wall. He groans as he climbs the ladder. There's a damp smell of earth and rotten wood. The yellowish kitchen light falls directly on top of us in the dark cellar. Like sunrays through a blanket of rain cloud, almost biblical. I hear a clunk as Father puts the rifle on the table, then he starts talking to Mother. I can't make out what they're saying, even though they're practically shouting. Then Father hauls up the ladder, closes the hatch, and secures it with a bolt. It's now pitch black in our dungeon. I hear the rug, then the dining table being pushed over the floorboards. Kneeling beside me, Boy touches my temple. "Are you OK, Juno?"

I nod, though my jaw is aching. "What happened?"

"Mother hit you because the photo album wasn't there anymore. As punishment they've locked us in the safe room. For five days. Mother said you've got to think where you put it."

"Five days?" I ask feebly. "We've got to get out of here, Boy."

"How are you going to do that?"

"I don't know yet."

"I'm really sorry, Juno," he whispers. "I didn't mean to get you into trouble."

"The album," I say. "Did you take it?"

Boy hesitates. "I couldn't believe what you'd told me." He sighs. "And when Father fell asleep in the chair, I secretly slipped down to the shed. You were right Juno, it's all true."

"So where's the album now?"

"Our sister's grave. Underneath the stone slab."

"Well done! They mustn't get hold of the album. It's our only chance of getting out of this alive. Because Mother wants it back at any price. She seems obsessed by this book. And if we–"

"You were right, Juno," Boy interrupts me. "I was kidnapped, too. I know my real name."

"Really?"

"Mikkel," he says faintly. "Mikkel Persson."

"Funny name," I say, then immediately regret it when I see his expression. "Sorry, Boy. I didn't mean that."

"I come from a country called Sweden. Ten years ago they took me from a children's nursery, in Göteborg, or something like that. That's what it said in the newspaper cuttings Mother stuck in the album."

"Sweden? That's the same country we're living in, Boy. Uncle Ole told me," I say, taking his hand. "You're from here, from Northland."

Unlike my sister Ruth, I wasn't there when they kidnapped their next victim. It was a golden autumn day and the migratory birds were gathering above the lake for their flight south. I was alone in the house with Mother and had been playing all afternoon with my dolly Mirabell in front of the fire. Later we had chicken broth for supper.

And a colorful comfort pill to celebrate the day, as Mother said. I slept soundly that fateful night when the full moon shone and Father came back to the island with our monthly groceries.

And Boy, his prey.

The next morning I saw this silent little stranger for the very first time when he sat opposite me at the breakfast table. The two-year-old wouldn't eat his porridge. Even though Mother had added blueberries and honey to it. I can't remember any more than that. So Boy was born in this area. That explains how Father was able to abduct him so quickly.

"Father didn't even notice that I'd gone."

"I'm not surprised. He was very drunk," I say.

"I was really careful when I ran out into the garden. Mother was in the kitchen making jelly. Comfort pills, I think. That's why she didn't see me."

"Her comfort pills," I say thoughtfully, sitting up. "I think Mother is planning to poison us. You must never swallow her new pills, understood?"

"What do you mean, poison?"

I suddenly have an idea. I get up, stumble with my arms in front of me toward the shelves with the supplies, and switch on the light. The bulb flickers, bathing our dungeon in dirty yellow light.

"Juno, what are you doing?" Boy whispers.

I take the first aid box off the shelf and put it on the sandy floor. Opening the lid, I push the bandaging, scissors, and syringes to one side.

And there it is, the orange tube of pills—our comfort pills. I unscrew the white cap and take out two large tablets. Squatting beside me, Boy watches intently. "What are you going to do with those?"

"These are placebos, Boy. Pills that have no effect."

"*Plasseeboes*? Why would Mother make pills that don't work?" he asks skeptically, then shakes his head. "It doesn't make sense."

"They were to practice with. To make us like eating them."

"Why, Juno? What are you going to do with these things?"

"It's just a precaution. If Mother forces us to swallow her new poison pills, we can take these ones," I say, putting the two amber pills beneath my wool jumper, in the front pocket of my dress. As I'm taking my left hand out again, my fingertips brush something smooth.

I'd forgotten all about it after the uproar in the shed with the disappearing album. My successful plan. At the very last moment I'd grabbed the thing from under the mattress after freeing myself from Mother on the landing to fetch my jumper.

"What…what is that?" Boy's eyes are open wide when he sees Luca's *cellulare* in my hand.

"Our connection to the guards," I reply, passing him the slim case. "It's called a *cellulare*. Luca secretly gave it to me so we could talk whenever we wanted. At eleven o'clock, they're coming to the shore to take us away."

"You mean you can talk with that?"

"Yes."

"Where do you put the lead in?"

"It doesn't need one."

"What about batteries?" he asks, twisting the shiny black device in his hands.

I shake my head. "I think it works without them."

"Turn it on, then, Juno! What are you waiting for?" He hands me the *cellulare* back.

I press the button beneath the glass surface and immediately the device beings to flicker. Colorful squares appear again. Boy blows through pursed lips in astonishment.

"I'll tell Luca we're locked in the cellar beneath the kitchen and can't come down to the shore. And that he's got to rescue us from here, OK?" I say, not pausing for breath. Pressing Luca's picture, I whisper, "Don't worry, Boy. Everything's going to be fine."

I hold the cold glass up to my ear.

And wait.

"Well?"

"It's not beeping."

"What?"

"I don't think it's working."

"What do you mean?"

"It's completely silent," I say, baffled. Taking the *cellulare* from my ear, I look at the glass, trying to find a solution. "It's always worked before," I say, in an attempt to reassure Boy. And then I spot the little numbers. The time in the top right-hand corner: 10:48.

Oh no! In twelve minutes Luca's going to arrive on the island, and we won't be at our agreed meeting place. What are we going to do now? Has that much time passed?

"Boy, we've got to get out of here now!"

"How?" he asks, sounding as nervous as me. "You have to notify the guards!"

"The thing's not working! And I don't know why!"

"Give it here!" Boy says, snatching the *cellulare* from my hand. He studies the colorful glass. "Is that Luca?" he asks, pointing at the photo of the boy with the black hair.

"Yes, you have to press it."

"But there's no button."

"Press the glass!"

"Oh." Boy taps the round picture and stares pensively at the glass.

"You have to put it to your ear or you won't hear anything," I explain. But instead Boy keeps moving the device around. He flips it over, lifts it up, higher, then lower again.

"What are you doing?" I ask, irritated. We don't have time for games.

"Something's moving," he says, very concentrated. "These four lines. Look, up by the edge. There are more if you hold the thing up."

I peer over his shoulder. He's right. One of the four dark-gray lines flickers. Boy shakes the *cellulare* like a carton of cream. "No idea what that means."

"Stay still," I hiss, trying to get the thing back.

"Ju-no?" The voice is broken and faint. "He-llo?"

"What was that?"

"Luca!" I say, pointing frantically at the device in Boy's hand. "It's working! Quick! Tell him we're down here in the cellar!"

"Hello?" Boy says, wide-eyed and holding the thing to his ear. A brief silence. "Yes, correct… Yes, Boy. I'm Juno's brother, we…" Silence again. Boy nods. "No, no, she's fine. We're in…" Boy's eyebrows knit together, and he raises his voice. "Hello? Hello? What problem? I can't hear…" He frantically waves the *cellulare* in the air, examines the glass surface, and puts it back to his ear. "Hello? Can you hear me?"

"Give it here!" I demand, standing right next to him. "Let me talk to Luca! We have to tell him that we can't—"

"No!" Boy snarls, yanking his arm backward. The little device goes flying in a wide arc toward the shelves where it crashes against a gas cartridge, and the colorful lights go out.

I look in horror at the broken device on the floor beside the shelves.

"What have you done?" I say, my voice quavering as I take little steps toward the *cellulare*. I bend down and pick up the warm object. The glass is broken—hairline cracks across the entire surface like a spider's web. I press the glass.

Nothing happens.

No lights, no squares.

"I...I'm sorry," Boy whispers beside me, his voice breaking. "I didn't mean to..."

I turn to my brother. He says nothing. Anger is boiling inside me; my eyes have narrowed to slits. I feel like going for his throat and strangling him until all the hopelessness has leaked from my body.

Instead I try to swallow my frustration, but barely succeed. I press the glass again and again and again. The device remains black.

"We've lost it, Boy! And all because of you. He's about to arrive on the island to rescue us! But we're not there. We're not at our agreed meeting place! Do you know what that means?" I take a deep breath and suppress the urge to gag that's creeping up my throat. "Father will shoot Luca. With his rifle! Luca is a stranger! And after that he'll kill us! Here in this dark hole. And it's all your fault. You've ruined everything."

Boy begins to sob.

I turn away from him and stare at the shattered device in my hand. Shattered hope.

It was all in vain.

Now tears are streaming down my burning cheeks, too, dripping on the broken device in my hand.

We're finished.

24

I squat by the stone wall with my legs bent, rocking from side to side in time with the whooshing in my ears. *They're going to kill us,* I tell myself over and over again; it's the only thought in my mind. Disheartened, I look up. Boy is pacing up and down, his arms crossed in front of his chest, all the while staring at the closed hatch.

It's hopeless. The trapdoor is bolted shut more than two meters above us, and we don't have a ladder.

"Mother and Father must have gone to bed," Boy whispers, pointing at the hatch. "It's completely quiet in the kitchen."

I let my head sink again. "That's irrelevant now."

"I could try giving you a leg up," Boy says.

"What then?" I ask. "How are we going to get through the trapdoor?"

"Maybe we could push it?"

"This is a safe room," I reply, exasperated. "From the strangers. Father built a fortress so nobody can get in."

"Not completely," Boy replies thoughtfully.

"What do you mean?"

"The rug," he says. "And the dining table."

I don't understand what he's getting at.

"The hiding place, Juno. Up in the kitchen. If the rug is over the hatch, the strangers don't know we're down here. And neither do the guards. That's why we always have to be very quiet during the practices, isn't it? But it's only camouflage. The bolt only holds the trapdoor in place."

"It's made out of thick wood," I say. "It makes no difference if there's a piece of material over it."

"Let's at least have a go."

"It's pointless, Boy."

I don't have the energy to argue with my brother. He just refuses to understand. I get up and pat the dust off my jumper. "Give it a rest. We've just got to resign ourselves to it, that's all. You destroyed Luca's *cellulare*, our only hope of being rescued. You can't make up for it now. We're trapped in here and that's that."

"What about Luca? Surely he'll come looking for us, won't he?" Boy whispers, undeterred by my accusations. "He'll come to our house if we're not down by the shore in a few minutes. Maybe he'll even sneak into the kitchen."

"And?"

"Well, there's no way we can shout for help, as that would just get Mother and Father's attention. But maybe there's another way," Boy says, taking a step toward me. "If we carefully shake the trapdoor, the rug under the table might move."

"What?"

"If Luca comes into the kitchen, he might notice the unusual folds in the rug. Then he'd discover the bolt and rescue us. I mean, he is a guard. He must look out for things like that. We can't give up!"

Anger rises within me. Not at Boy, but at myself. The hopeless situation with the broken *cellulare* got me so disheartened that I stopped hoping. I stopped fighting. My somber thoughts paralyzed me.

"I'm sorry, Boy," I say softly, putting my hand on his shoulder. "You're absolutely right. We can't give up. It's not over yet."

Boy gives a sympathetic nod, a film of dampness shimmering on his cheeks. "I'm sorry, too, Juno. It was my mistake." Then he clasps his hands and gestures at me. "Whatever happens, me and you have to stick together. We're still brother and sister, aren't we? Right. Get up, now!"

I put one foot on his hands, push myself up on his shoulder, and listen. In the kitchen above me it's quiet. It seems as if Mother and Father aren't downstairs. Maybe they've gone to bed. I stretch my arms upward, balancing on Boy's hands.

My fingertips touch the cold wood. I cautiously press both hands against the hatch, gently shaking the boards. I can hear the metallic rattling of the bolt.

"Harder!" Boy whispers from below.

I breathe, focus, and press harder. The rattling gets louder.

"Even harder!"

"We can't be so loud," I whisper back.

"But the rug has to move!"

"I get that," I snap, hitting the wood with greater irritation than I'd intended. The bolt clanks, echoing through our tiled kitchen.

"Hurry up! I can't hold you much longer."

I push the hatch again. It creaks.

"More!" Boy cries. "You've got to push harder."

"Yes, yes!" I say, hammering the boards as hard as I can. The noise must be audible in the hallway. I've no idea if I've moved the rug.

"And? Is it working?"

"I don't know!"

"Try again!"

Suddenly I'm overcome by doubt about whether our plan's going to work. How can it? Shaking the hatch is silly; it's never going to shift the rug. It's merely wishful thinking. A stupid, childish plan.

Furious at our naivety, I thrash the trapdoor with my left fist. And again. Harder and harder. I let all my bottled-up frustration out on the wooden boards. The hinges rattle.

"Not so loud, Juno!"

Boy and me have to stick together. We've got to get out of here, I bellow in my thoughts, drumming wildly on the wood. I don't care anymore if Mother and Father can hear the crashing in their bedroom. There's so much pent-up anger and fear inside me, now being offloaded via my fists. What's Mother planning to do with us? I don't want to die! Open the oven door, you old witch!

"For God's sake, Juno! What are you doing?" Boy hisses.

I notice the hinges, which clatter tinnily against each other with every blow. They make a hellish racket; I push harder. With every ounce of my strength. And suddenly I notice the little rod, the thin metal pin. My shaking has forced it slightly out of the rusty hinge.

"I can't hold you anymore," Boy says, sliding me down.

"The hinge," I pant, out of breath, when my feet are back on the ground. A spark of hope glimmers inside me. "The pin from one of the hinges has loosened a bit. That could be our chance!" I point my bandaged hand at the rusty piece of metal. "If we get those pins out, we can push the hatch open."

"How are you going to do that?"

"We just need something thin and hard," I reply. "And a hammer."

The bulb above us flickers. Boy looks around the cellar. There's not much here apart from Father's wingback chair. The wooden shelves with the jars of preserves, the open first aid box with Mother's comfort pills, fifteen canisters of water, the gas cooker, sacks of potatoes, and a pile of wool blankets.

"Father doesn't keep any tools down here, Juno." Boy sounds crushed. "They're all in the shed."

"Maybe we'll find something else," I say, standing by the shelves. I take an apple and hand it to my brother; preoccupied, he bites into it. I need a moment to myself; I have to concentrate. Boy will be busy with the apple for a few minutes, and I can think in peace. My gaze wanders across the bottles of high-percentage alcohol, the box of long candles, the matches, the pickled fish in jam jars. And then the green plastic box at my feet. I kneel down and rummage through the contents: bandages, pills, scissors, syringes.

"Found anything?" Boy says, his mouth full.

"Uh-huh," I say, grabbing the little scissors. "Maybe." Might they work? No, the blades are too short. I return them to the box. A syringe? Perhaps: the length of the cannula might be right. The thick needle is made of metal.

We've got to try it.

Tearing open the protective film, I attach the cannula to the plastic syringe and put it on the floor in front of me.

"Would you help me?" I say to Boy, and we drag the heavy chair beneath the trapdoor.

"Why didn't we use this before?" Boy gasps. I suddenly hear footsteps. And voices—just a few meters above us in the kitchen!

"Shhh!" I hiss anxiously, pointing up at the hatch. Boy understands at once and shuts up. Nervously clinging to the back of the chair, we stare up at the hatch. Any second they're going to open it and see us. And the armchair: our escape plan.

"I told you it was nothing," I hear Father say. Through the hatch it sounds muffled. He paces up and down clumsily.

"What about the noise?" Mother asks. "It was coming from the kitchen."

"There's a big storm brewing. It might have been a gust of air clattering the window."

Our eyes remain fixed on the hatch. I hold my breath.

"Maybe we ought to check on the children," Mother says. Her footsteps come closer, stopping right above us.

"How are they going to open the hatch?" Father says. "From down there?" His footsteps labor back to the kitchen door. "Come on; let's go back to bed. They'll be duly punished tomorrow. Today was just a foretaste. They'll soon tell us where they've hidden our album."

We hear the kitchen light being switched off. Footsteps in the hall, on the stairs, the bedroom door.

Then it's quiet again.

Boy and I look at each other. Neither of us dares speak. But we don't have to, either. I can tell he's thinking the same as me: what punishment was Father talking about? I'd rather not find out.

With the syringe between my teeth I carefully climb onto the seat of the chair, put one foot on the arm, then climb onto the backrest. Boy holds my legs tight so I don't fall off. Then I put the needle to the pin and press as hard as I can. But it won't budge. Not a millimeter.

"Well?" Boy whispers from below.

"The needle's too thin!" I sigh as I force all my weight against the cannula. Metal scrapes against metal, sweat pours down my face. "It has to—" All of a sudden the pin shifts. A little way, at least two centimeters, into the hinge. "It's working," I call out relieved. "Boy! The pin! It's moving!"

Then the needle breaks.

With a screech, the needle slides across the metal hinge and bores itself into the forefinger of my bandaged hand. In shock I lose my balance and squeal as I topple onto the chair. My head hits the backrest.

"Juno! Juno!" Boy calls out, waving his arms in a panic and staring at the syringe sticking out of my hand. I can't feel any pain. It must be the shock, I think, gaping at Boy's contorted moon face. I feel as if I'm in a sort of dream. His skin is ashen, his eyes wide open. His mouth is stammering words I can't understand.

"It's alright, Boy," I say weakly, once my heart has calmed down. "I'm fine."

My brother shakes his head, still pointing with trembling fingers at the syringe in my hand. The broken needle has thrust itself right through the bandage.

"It doesn't hurt," I say, to calm him down. And that's the truth. "Look, it isn't bleeding."

"How come?" he asks.

I nervously grip the needle with my left hand, intent on pulling it out. Closing my eyes, I prepare myself for a torrent of blood. I pull very slowly, very carefully. But it doesn't work. I pull the cannula harder, but it doesn't move. Like something was holding onto it.

"What's wrong?" Boy asks. I open my eyes.

"The needle's stuck."

"What do you mean? In the bone?" Boy asks, an expression of disgust on his face.

I shrug and wipe my brow with my sleeve. I'm going to try again. But this time with my eyes open. Gritting my teeth, I pull on the cannula, still feeling no pain. Maybe Boy's right, maybe it really has gone into the bone of my finger?

A determined jerk.

And finally it works. I've pulled the broken needle from my finger. It was easier than I thought.

"You didn't even scream," Boy says with a hint of admiration.

"I'm as surprised as you are," I say, waiting for the bandage to become soaked by blood.

"Is it a deep wound?"

"No idea."

"We need to disinfect the puncture with alcohol right away," Boy says. He scurries over to the shelves and picks up a brown glass bottle as I carefully unwrap the bandage from my hand.

"It might sting," Boy says, when he squashes onto the chair beside me. I remove the last layer and look at my milky-white finger: not a drop of blood. The pencil rolls onto my legs. Removing the bottle top, Boy asks, "Which finger was it, then?" He looks at me expectantly, shaking the alcohol in his hand. "Juno? Where's the puncture?"

"Here," I say, pointing at the little hole in the pencil. "Right here."

Boy frowns. "The needle dug into the pencil?" He breathes a sigh of relief. "Really? You're bloody lucky."

I shake my head. "No, Boy," I say, twiddling the pencil between my fingers. "*We're* bloody lucky, do you understand?" Boy looks at me, confused. The solution to our problems was right under our noses. "We can push the pins out with this!" The pencil is thin and strong enough.

"What?"

I clamber straight back onto the backrest. "We've got to hurry. Bring me the gas cartridge, quick!"

"What are you going to do with that?"

"Use it as a hammer! Now come on!"

"But it might explode!"

"It's the only solid object in the cellar. I'll be careful." I point at the shelves and say, "Go on! What are you waiting for?"

Boy fetches the cartridge and throws it to me. I catch it with both hands and quickly wrap my bandage around the metal tin.

"Why are you doing that?"

"It'll make less noise," I say, climbing higher. Finally, I feel in my element. "Hold me tightly!"

Concentrating hard, I put the pencil to the pin of the hinge like a nail and whack it as hard as I can. There's a hollow *clunk* as the pin shoots several centimeters out of the hinge. "Boy, it's working!" I hammer the cartridge against the pencil again. Bit by bit the pin works free and falls to the ground with a clatter.

"Father was right!" Boy beams. "You really are an expert planner!"

Feeling faintly proud of myself, I put the pencil against the other hinge and start hammering again. It takes just a few blows for the second metal pin to come out, too.

We've done it.

"Push the trapdoor open!" Boy whispers as I continue holding up the wooden flap with both hands. Standing on tiptoe, I push as hard as I can. The trapdoor moves, I push even higher and feel the weight of the rug. Then the door finally comes off its hinges.

"Can you take it off me?" I call out quietly. Boy lets go of my legs and holds his arms up. I start to wobble perilously and have to balance carefully to avoid falling from the chair. I pass Boy the heavy trapdoor, which he takes with both hands and leans against the wall while I clasp the opening in the kitchen floor.

"Well done!" Boy says.

Now we just have to somehow climb into the kitchen. With my left hand, I push the rug up; this is child's play compared to the solid wooden hatch. Dust sprinkles onto my face. My nose begins to itch, but I mustn't sneeze now. I keep pushing the material away until finally I can see the underside of our dining table.

I thrust myself off the armchair with both legs and with my arms pull myself through the narrow opening.

I've made it into the kitchen. Exhausted, I roll onto my back and close my eyes for a second.

I listen to the ticking of the clock.

"Juno!" I hear Boy whisper. "Help me up!"

Flipping over onto my stomach I hold out my right hand to him in the cellar. Boy grabs it and pulls himself up. We hug. Briefly and feebly.

Then we push the rug back over the dark hole in the floor, lift the table and put it back down on the patterned material to make it taut. One last check. Yes, that should work. Until morning, Mother and Father will never notice that we're no longer captive in the dungeon. And if they do, we'll long be on the other side of the lake by then. I glance at the cat clock above the fridge: 11:04.

"We did it, Boy!" I whisper, unbolting the door to the vegetable garden. A damp wind blows into the kitchen. It's started to rain. The rumbling of thunder.

I take my brother by the hand. "Come on! It's time to leave this nightmare island before they realize!"

Boy gives me a weary nod and then we run outside.

Our hearts beat wildly as we head for freedom.

25

The rain pelts down relentlessly as we speed across the muddy lawn. I keep looking up at the horizon; the sluggish storm clouds drift across the lake like ghosts in mourning dress. Raindrops the size of bilberries slap my face; I wipe the water out of my eyes. The wool jumper sticks to my skin just like my hair.

"Quicker, Juno! Run!"

We race across the vegetable patch, hand in hand, past the two loudspeaker masts, the well, our tool shed. Our eyes remain fixed on our goal: the shore, where we'll be rescued.

I turn around. All of the windows in the cabin are pitch black, clouds of mist reflecting in the dark panes of glass. An eerie chill grips my entire body. In the gloomy dusk, our house looks like a troll's skull, hurling curses at us as we escape. The house has never looked like this before. I'm overjoyed to be leaving it—finally. One last glance up at the second floor, to my bedroom.

I hear a dull rumble of thunder, like two rocks rolling into one another. It smells of damp earth, pine, sweet blossoms, and moss. I stumble over a fern but manage to steady myself. My hands are full of mud. Another thunderclap. I jump. For a second or two, everything is brightly lit. The sky, trees, our house. Was that a shadow at the window?

Is there someone standing at my window?

"Is that him? Down there?" Boy cries over the thunder, tearing me from my thoughts. He waves his hands at the black dinghy lying hidden in the tall reeds.

"Yes!" I say with relief, running after my brother, who vaults a tree stump several meters ahead of me. "That's Luca!" It seems like a dream. Only twenty minutes ago, locked in our dungeon, I thought I'd never see him again.

Never give up, Juno! There's always a way!

Luca gives us a sign with his flashlight. The hood is pulled down over his head. Just a few hundred meters to go. With the rain still bucketing down, he turns back, stretches a plastic sheet over the boat, and secures it with rope. The raindrops that hit it spring in all directions like a swarm of startled grasshoppers, accompanied by a sort of drumroll.

Boy reaches the boat first. Luca offers him his hand, which Boy takes tentatively and shakes. I fall around Luca's neck, squeezing him as hard as I can. I feel his heart beating. Freeing himself from the embrace he looks at me with his dark-brown eyes. I'm suddenly hot all over. I've been longing for this moment.

"I can't tell you how much I've missed you," I whisper.

Luca gives me a strained smile, and brushes a wet lock of hair from his brow.

"Why are you on your own?" Boy asks, looking puzzled. "Where are the others? The other guards?"

"There was a change of plan," Luca says quietly. Something seems to be weighing on his mind. "The scheduled attack was postponed."

"What does that mean?"

"It was aborted. Because of the storm. No visibility. For the divers and the helicopter. My *capo* postponed the attack...till tomorrow." Luca is visibly nervous. "I came here on my own because I knew you were expecting to be rescued at eleven o'clock. I couldn't get through to you by phone. And the risk that your kidnappers would–"

"Does that mean the other guards don't...know you're on the island?" Boy stammers. Luca doesn't reply.

"Are you going to get badly punished for this?" I ask, concerned. Luca and I have more in common than I thought. When we're fixed on a goal, we have to achieve it. No matter how severe the punishment. It's just what we're like. And Luca did it for me. Like a brave prince with wings.

"I don't work anymore for..." Luca says, breaking off as he shines the flashlight on the boat in the reeds. "Get in the boat first!" I nod and put one foot over the rim. Taking my arm, Luca steadies me as I climb over the air-filled tube, then he helps Boy get in.

"So you're Elly's little brother?"

"Yes, Boy."

"His real name is Mikkel," I add, sitting on the narrow wooden board. "He was kidnapped here in Sweden."

"Scandinavia, I understand. My colleagues will check that later." Luca seems to think about this for a moment, craning his neck into the sky. Rain flows down his slim nose and he opens his mouth. "Boy, *naturalmente*. That explains your unusual name." Then he turns back to us. "We ought to hurry. Let's go!"

"Unusual, how?" Boy asks, sitting beside me on the bench. "What do you mean?"

"The Swedish word for a boy is *pojke*. That sounds like Boy," Luca says. "Maybe your kidnappers didn't know how to talk to you in Swedish and that's why they called you Boy." Luca is still standing in the reeds, looking around watchfully. "It would be better if you lay flat on the bottom of the boat so nobody can see you."

"Father abducted him from a nursery," I say, kneeling and sliding toward my brother on my tummy beneath the black tarpaulin. "Boy was only two then."

"How do you know all of this?" Luca says, untying the knot securing the boat to a rock.

"I read a newspaper article about when I went missing," Boy calls out from under the tarpaulin. "In a German newspaper. It was stuck in Mother's photo album."

"*Bene*, very good," Luca says, jumping into the boat. "When we're at the hotel, you can tell the police everything." He takes hold of the paddles fixed to the sides. "The main thing is that I get you to safety!"

An indescribable feeling of liberation permeates my entire body. *To safety*. Tears well in my eyes.

"Right, then. Stay down there. Understood? We mustn't take any risks. Nobody must see us on the lake," Luca whispers, sitting on the bench in front of us. The boat rocks gently from side to side. The puddles at his feet turn into minor tidal waves.

My jumper becomes soaked with water.

Boy and I hold hands and nod encouragingly at each other, in tense anticipation of breaking our seventh and most important commandment: *we're leaving the island.*

But Luca hesitates. He sits on the bench, not moving. We stare at his drenched back. And wait. More thunder, lightning. For a second

Luca's hunched torso is brightly illuminated; his silhouette has similarities with our big rock. Then it's dark again.

Luca appears to be mulling over something; he pushes his hood forward and back. Thick fog is gathering. I'm starting to freeze.

"Go, go! What are you waiting for?" Boy snarls impatiently beside me. "We've got to get out of here!"

"Shut up, Boy!" I say. How can my little brother be so embarrassing? Luca's helping us. He'll have his reasons for waiting. Maybe he's seen or heard something unusual in the distance. We'll be off in a minute for sure. Even though I also wish we'd go now. Before I get even more scared.

"*Un momento*," Luca says, letting go of the oars again. Then he turns to us and bends down below the tarp. "Where is it? The album. I hope you brought it with you. We'll need it as evidence."

"The photo album?" Boy says, not understanding. "Why?"

"*Sì*, the book. All the evidence. Do you have it?"

"I'm afraid not," I say, wiping the rain from my eye. I'm annoyed at myself. I'd promised it to Luca. "I'm sorry, we didn't have the time. Mother locked us in the safe room. But...Boy hid it well."

"*Merda!*" The expression on Luca's face changes. "But Elly, I told you that—"

"Don't worry," Boy interrupts him. "The book's in a safe place. Mother will never find it. I put it beneath a gravestone," he explains proudly. "Our sister's gravestone."

"Ruth's," I add.

Luca jerks his head. I can see the anger rising in him. "Out here on the island?"

"Yes, why?" Boy asks. "You can fetch it later."

"*Maledetto!*" Luca looks horrified. "It's raining! Jesus, look at that!" He says, demonstratively craning his neck into the pouring sky and shaking it. "The rain will destroy all the paper! Evidence is being lost by the minute! Why couldn't you have found a better hiding place? But now it's too late—we have to go!"

"But there's only pictures in it," Boy says.

I sense that Luca is furious. He turns from side to side, running a hand through his wet hair. "Maybe they kidnapped other children apart from you! The album would have given us certainty! And besides, it's evidence if the kidnappers deny the other crimes. Did you see other photographs of missing children in it?"

I hadn't thought of that. I didn't look beyond Ruth. "I…I don't know, no." Boy shakes his head guiltily, too.

"So what are we going to do now?" I ask hesitantly.

"First of all I'm going to get you over to the other side!"

"I could go and fetch it quickly," Boy says, pointing to the dark path up to the trees. "The grave is right there!"

"No!" Luca says. "Too dangerous. It's more important that I get you to safety now. We don't have time for the album."

"But it's just a few meters!" Boy says, crawling out from beneath the tarpaulin. "Honestly. It's right behind that copse!"

"Stay here!" Luca says, trying to grab Boy's sleeve, who's already got both legs over the edge of the boat.

"No, it was my fault," Boy says, shaking Luca's hand off. "And I'm going to make up for it. I'll be back in a sec!"

"For God's sake," Luca curses, hauling my brother back into the boat. "What's got into you?"

Boy falls onto his back and yelps. Then he stares at Luca wide-eyed, rubbing his forearm.

"*Va bene allora*," Luca says. "Just a few meters, you say?" Boy nods. Luca gets to his feet. "*Porca madonna!* The two of you are going to wait here in the boat." Then he climbs over the side and into the thick reeds. "I'll fetch the evidence, and then we'll get away from here, *avete capito*?"

Reaching under his jumper, Luca pulls something black from a leather holster. A pistol. "Stay in the boat! Under the tarpaulin. And not a sound, not even a whisper, *intesi*? I'll be back very soon!"

We nod.

"Please be careful," I whisper as Luca disappears into the reeds. I watch him for a few seconds, then Boy and I creep back beneath the tarp.

We lie flat on the wet bottom and wait.

The rain continues to hammer down incessantly on the plastic cover over us. It crackles like our record player when the disc has finished playing. A cold wind cuts into my face.

"Are you in love with this guy?" Boy says.

"What?"

"Are you in love with him?"

"No, rubbish!" I snap. I'm grateful he can't see my cheeks in the darkness. I bet they're glowing like a sunset. "Luca's a guard."

"And he's ancient."

"No, he isn't!"

"The main thing is that he finds the album," Boy whispers. "It would've been better if I'd gone."

We fall silent. And wait. Somewhere in the woods there's a flash of lightning. A clap of thunder. The minutes don't seem to pass. How long has Luca been gone? I prop myself up on my elbows. My wool jumper has soaked up the water like a sponge. I'm shivering.

"I hope he finds the grave."

"You can't miss the cross," I say.

"It's dark, Juno. And foggy," Boy whispers. "Anyway, he's been gone too long. Ten minutes, at least."

My stomach cramps. He's right. Both of us know where Ruth's grave is. Hidden behind the two birch trees. But will Luca find it? He doesn't know this part of the island. I hope he didn't go the wrong way. Otherwise he'll miss Ruth's grave and head straight for our house. I can't help thinking of the spooky shadow at my bedroom window. What if I didn't imagine it?

Boy slides closer to me and whispers, "It's OK, Juno. Don't worry. He's a guard."

My entire body is shivering. But not from cold. Boy must have noticed and places a hand on my back. "Luca's going to find the album. Don't forget he's got a flashlight. And a gun."

I snuggle up to my brother and let him cuddle me. We lie still like that for several minutes, our eyes closed and dreaming of the other side. The rain continues to pound the tarpaulin; it's soothing.

Then we hear a muffled bang in the distance.

26

I flinch. A swarm of birds screeches as they flap above our heads and fly off. Boy clutches my arm and presses himself more tightly against my back. Now he's shaking, too, as if armies of ants were marching across his body.

I wriggle free of his embrace and from the depths of my lungs, I yell Luca's name.

"Stay here!" Boy shouts.

"But we've got to help him!"

"No! We should wait here, Juno!"

Boy tugs my jumper, tries to hold me back. I do my best to stifle my growing panic, but it doesn't work.

"I'm sure that was just thunder," Boy soothes me, rubbing my arm mechanically, as if he were cleaning a window. It hurts. "A lightning strike, very close by, some big tree. It's all going to be fine, Juno. Please quiet down!"

"No, it was a shot!" I scream at him and try to crawl out from under the tarpaulin. Raindrops bombard my forehead. "You know it was, Boy. Someone fired a shot!"

"Listen, Luca will be back very soon!" he says, grabbing my knuckles. "Give him time. Another few minutes!"

I fall back onto my stomach, feeling tense and taking shallow breaths through my mouth. It could have been lightning, yes, maybe, I think, trying to reassure myself. Even though I know better.

When I roll onto my side an oar digs into me. I push it against the side of the boat and look at the stormy sky above. A black whirl of cloud, like paint in a glass of water. OK, we'll wait.

Luca's bound to be back soon, the photo album under his arm. He'll row us to the other side of the lake. The police will take us in and bring us back to our parents, our real parents. I try to imagine what my home in England might look like. A little house with a garden. The sun is shining. There are two fruit trees in front of it, it smells of spring and freshly mown grass. A narrow sandy path leads up to a red front door. Maybe they've got a little dog. Or a kitten. I picture myself stroking it on the steps. Velvety-soft fur. The baby cat purrs. Then there's another loud, sharp bang. There's a third one shortly afterward.

The shot shatters my reverie. They echo across the lake for several seconds.

"Luca!" I call out, shaking myself out of my state of shock. I leap up and clamber over the side of the boat. Boy tries again to grab my foot, but I shake him off. "Those were shots! Gunshots!"

"Don't go," Boy urges. "It's too dangerous!"

"But he might need our help!" I cry.

"No, *we* need *his* help, Juno! Let's row to the other side, it's our only chance!"

"But we can't leave him on his own! He's risked everything for us!" Tears are streaming down my cheeks. "He might be injured."

"Or already dead," Boy shouts back. "Juno, we've got to get out of here! At once!"

How can he say something like that? After everything Luca's done for us. I shake my head in disgust and run off. I just run off. Battle my way through the shoulder-height reeds without once turning around. My shoes sink into the sludge. It becomes more difficult by the step. My lungs are burning. The dress is sticking to my body. I climb over the rotting tree stump, leap across an elder bush and hurry across the boggy meadow until I finally get to the two birch trees. Boy's angry cries are no longer audible.

My sister's grave. It's there, just a few meters away. I turn in every direction and breathe slowly through my half-open mouth. The garden is dark and deserted. Nobody to be seen. Not Father, not Mother. And not Luca, either. I stare at the flat gravestone amongst the wildflowers. It lies in its place, untouched. Raindrops bounce off the grayish-black surface. Luca appears to have missed it in the dark. Where on earth is he? I look all around me again, unable to see any footprints. The rain has washed them away. Luca must have passed this way, right? An owl hoots in the far distance. I'm alone. Cautiously I creep over to Ruth's grave, push my fingers into the wet mud and heave up the heavy stone.

Mother's photo album—it's still there, thank God! I pull it out and stuff it under my itchy jumper. It's barely wet; only at the corners has the paper curled slightly. Luca will be proud of me. If only I knew where he was. I hide behind a hawthorn bush and look around. Only darkness and the rumble of thunder overhead. Once more I think of the shots. Were they fired from a pistol or a rifle? I can't tell. That was the loudest bang I've ever heard, even during a storm. I wince. I hope Luca wasn't shot. Please, dear God, let him live. He's the only person I still trust.

I kneel on the muddy earth and put my hands together. Close my eyes. Please let everything be OK, I pray over and over again. *Yea, though I walk through the valley of the shadow of death, I will fear no evil, for Thou art with me; Thy rod and Thy staff, they comfort me.*

There's a sudden flash of lightning, and I open my eyes again. It's hit an old spruce tree quite close. A bough cracks and falls to the ground. It must be a sign from God. Luca's alive!

Swallowing my worry, I get up and wipe the mud from my legs. I have to get back to the boat at once. Luca might already be back at the shore, waiting for me.

I look at my sister's wooden cross one last time.

Take care!

Then I do a double take when I notice the hole that's been dug not far from her grave. When I approach it, I see it's at least two meters deep. When was that dug? And why?

As I'm remembering the punishment we heard Father talking about this morning, a siren starts wailing out of the blue. In shock, I stare up at the house, rooted to the spot. The howling of the loudspeaker masts buzzes in my ears like a swarm of mosquitoes, and an inner voice pulls me down into the safe room. Strangers on the island! Strangers like me.

Shaking myself from my paralysis, I get my legs into gear. I run, faster and faster, clutching the album tightly beneath my jumper. Now I barely feel the rain anymore. I struggle through the reeds and over fallen trees, bushes, and branches. Wet hair hangs down over my face. I push a birch branch to one side, leap over a rock by the shore... and freeze. The dinghy.

It's gone!

In a panic, I look around everywhere for it. It was right here, I'm certain of that. The imprint of Luca's dinghy is clearly visible. Even though the rain has washed away our footprints as if we'd never been here, the drag marks of the boat lead down to the water. Have Luca and Boy escaped the island without me? I raise my head and scan the lake.

The moon behind the storm clouds, high above the woods, bathes everything in a dark-blue, magical light. Millions of raindrops strike the surface of the water like a shower of meteorites, forming millions of circles on the lake. I peer more closely. Over there! Is that something moving? A black dot, like a paddling beetle, a few hundred meters away on the water. It's the boat, Luca's dinghy! Boy is rowing away from the island. Without me. He drags the oars through the water with calm, fluid movements. I wave at him with both my arms, but he doesn't appear to see me. He just rows on regardless.

"Boy!" I call out across the lake. "I'm here! Here!" But it's hopeless; he's too far away, and the sirens are too loud. All the same, I mustn't give up. I shout again, cupping both hands to my mouth and yelling his name as loud as I can.

Boy stops and looks up.

Taking out the album from beneath my jumper I wave it in the air like a flag. "I've got it! Come back!" Now Boy waves back at me, thrusting his arms high. He shouts something, but I can't understand him.

"What? I can't hear you, Boy!" I yell back.

His arm movements become more frenetic, his shouting louder. He keeps pointing in my direction, now with both arms, as if trying to shoo away a flock of birds.

"Come back! I've got Mother's album," I cry, beckoning him back. Why couldn't he wait for me?

Crossing his arms above his head, Boy bellows across the lake, but all I hear are fragments of words: "*Ru...ay...ick!*"

I shrug and shake my head blankly. It makes no sense at this distance. Trying one last time, I shout, "What did you say? Boy, please come back!"

Then I hear a crack a few meters behind me. Like the breaking of a brittle branch. No, not wood—more metallic than that. The image of our safe room flashes in my mind. The armchair, the ladder on the wall, a familiar sound. A hollow sound like a rifle being loaded. Terrified, I whip around.

My worst nightmare has come true. A blow to my stomach; I feel sick. Father. He's standing in front of me menacingly, holding his rifle. Now I understand Boy's frantic waving; he was trying to warn me.

"Where's your brother going?" Father mutters, cocking his head and staring at the lake behind me. Strands of his wet hair hang over his glasses.

"Boy?" I gasp. "That's not..." My voice fails.

"All these years we've been protecting you," Father says, wiping the rain from his glasses with his sleeve.

"Father, please. Let us go!"

"Nobody's going to leave this island and tell on us," Father says, raising the rifle to his eyes and aiming at the little dinghy. "Not even your brother."

27

Now everything happens very fast. Without thinking about it, I raise my arm and hurl the photo album at Father. It hits him square in the face. The rifle jolts to the right and a shot is fired, resounding across the lake. A fountain of water splashes up just a few meters from Boy's boat.

"What are you doing?" Father growls, wiping the blood from his cheek. It's been cut by the sharp edge of the album. He rubs his eyes in astonishment, smearing blood over his forehead.

"My glasses," he stammers. "Where the hell are they?"

The *Book of Consolation* knocked the glasses off his nose. Without them he's practically blind. This is my chance. I scour the wet ground. Stretching his arms out in front of him, Father flounders through the reeds and screams, "Juno! Where are you? Help me!"

Desperately I comb the reeds. The glasses must be here somewhere! I take a few steps toward the muddy shore: stones, rocks, grass, roots. If I find them before Father does, there's a chance I might get out of this alive. Spotting something shiny, I bend down.

Is that…? No, just a broken reed, glinting damply in the moonlight. Keep looking! I push some ferns aside—nothing, no glasses. Hurry up! Out of the corner of my eye I see Father putting the rifle to his shoulder again. He swings it around aimlessly. "I know you're still here!"

Throwing myself on the ground, I lie there motionless. My heart is racing. I try to keep as still as possible, taking shallow breaths through my mouth. I warily lift my head and see Father trudging through the reeds, his rifle at the ready.

"Come on, Juno; let's talk about it. We'll talk about whatever you want," he calls out in all directions. "That was just a warning shot. To stop your brother from rowing over to the strangers. You understand? Come on out, now."

I hold my breath. Then he bends down and lays the rifle on a rock. What's he doing?

"Did you see that?" Father says, putting both hands above his head. "I don't want to hurt you. You're our daughter. Come and help me look."

I don't believe a word he's saying.

Turning back to the water, I scrutinize the shore. Nothing but stones everywhere. Blades of grass. There's no letup in the rain. I feel cold, and my jumper is stiff and crusty. I move deeper into the wet reeds. The glasses must have landed here somewhere. Father is shouting, breaking through the undergrowth just a few meters behind me. His footsteps are getting closer. I don't know if he's picked the rifle up again, nor do I have time to think about it. Keep searching!

Then, finally, I spot the glasses between the oval leaves of an arrowhead plant. They're in the mud just an arm's length away!

I bend down quickly and grab them with both hands. Water splashes everywhere, and I swallow sludge.

"Have you found them?" the deep voice asks. Startled, I roll over onto my back. He's standing over me, swaying like a birch tree in the storm and blinking at me.

"Give them here!" he hisses.

In desperation I look from side to side. There's no escape; Father's blocking my way. I look past him and see the rifle still on the rock.

Flipping back onto my tummy, I propel myself into the ice-cold lake and swim, thrashing my arms and legs about like a frog. But soon I'm out of breath, and my clothes are dragging me under. When I resurface, snorting, I hear Father shouting agitatedly behind me and I turn around.

He wades toward me through the knee-deep bog until he suddenly topples into the water headfirst. He can't have seen where he was going. Rowing wildly with his arms, he swims in my direction as if he's coming to save me. But the opposite is true. I speed up my stroke, pushing as hard as I can with my legs, but progress is slow as I can't open my left hand. Still clutching Father's glasses, I pull my left fist through the water as energetically as I can.

"Where are you going, Juno? You're going to drown. You can't swim!" I hear Father pant behind me. He's laboring his way through the water, clearly impeded by all that alcohol and his blurred vision. He's paddling uncoordinatedly in all directions. I look left and right, wondering which way to swim. I'll never make it to the other side, especially not in the wool jumper and summer dress that are weighing my body down like lead. I can't see Boy and the dinghy anywhere, either. Thick swathes of fog drift across the churned-up surface of the water. Swimming out this far was a mistake.

"Give me my bloody glasses!" Father splutters. "Where are you?" He turns around, flailing his arms and legs, his movements getting ever more cumbersome. He swallows water, coughs, but I'm never going to hand him back the glasses. They give me a feeling of power, power over my father.

Again I find myself thinking of Thumbelina and her escape from the wicked toad. Then I have an idea. My survival instinct has been awakened. I could trick Father into swimming to the middle of the lake then secretly glide past him underwater. But it's more than ten meters to the shore, and I don't swim well. Let alone underwater. But I've got to try; I have no other option.

"I'll give them back if you tell me why you abducted us," I shout with the last of my strength to lure him toward me.

Father lurches in my direction and scans the lake. "Haven't you always been happy with us?" he yells back. Then he starts swimming briskly in my direction. "Juno," he gasps, "come over here! I'll tell you everything when we're back on land." He sounds on the brink of exhaustion.

Another bank of fog drifts across the lake. Now is the right moment! Taking a deep breath I dive under the water and swim away as fast as I can. I have to strain every muscle; it feels as if dozens of creepers have wrapped themselves around my feet. I kick harder, and my lungs begin to burn. One more stroke, and another. I open my eyes—everything is black. Fire is shooting through my veins. Another one. Then I'm out of breath, and I have to return to the surface.

I gasp for air and just manage to suppress a cough. Very carefully I go back under as far as the tip of my nose and turn around. I can't see Father anywhere. Raindrops splash in the water, creating circles, and there's thunder.

Then I hear Father calling. In the distance, at least twenty meters away. He sounds weak and monosyllabic. I take care as I swim back to the shore. There's a flash of lightning above the woods, lighting up the steep rock ahead of me where I drew the picture of the tall houses. Then it immediately falls dark again. I keep swimming toward our big rock where Uncle Ole almost glimpsed me just a few days ago. Did I really go so far from where I entered the water? I continue to toil with my strokes, swallowing ice-cold water, until I finally feel the boggy ground beneath my fingers. Slippery stones and mud. I've reached the shore.

Shattered, I climb out of the water and slide down against the big rock. My jumper is sticking to my skin. I did it; I left Father behind. My plan worked. I wrap my arms around my legs, my entire body frozen. From time to time the moon appears between the black storm clouds, tinting the water a dark-blue color.

I listen to the night. The rain crackles like an open fire, and I hear the odd quack of a duck. But nothing from Father. No more cries. Maybe he's swum further out into the lake or has lost the strength to shout. Has he drowned? I rack my brains over what to do now, but I don't leave the lake out of my sight for one moment.

The dinghy has gone. And with it, Boy. I hope he's safely reached the other side.

I can't get off the island. It's too far to swim and somewhere out there on the lake Father is looking for me.

Rain runs down the back of my neck. I shiver. Through the ghostly silhouettes of the birch trees I spy our log cabin.

The light is on in the kitchen. It was dark before, wasn't it? Maybe Mother switched it on? To sound the siren, which is still wailing in the darkness. Is she waiting in the house for Father to return? I look at his glasses still in my hand.

I've got to find Luca before Father comes back to kill me. Again I turn to the lake and scope the surface of the water, but my view is blocked by a curtain of fog. What am I going to do? I need a weapon to defend myself. I look on the ground for a large stone and then remember Father's rifle. He left it on a rock. I could fetch it, but that would mean going all the way back to the reeds. It's too risky, as Father might have returned to the shore. I'd be trapped. No, I need something else. And quickly. As I'm mulling this over, I gaze back up at the kitchen window. Like the eye of a troll, open wide. A knife, I think, getting to my feet. I could creep behind the house and hide beneath the window. Wait until Mother comes into the garden to look for Father. Then I could slip inside, open the cutlery drawer, and arm myself with a knife.

A hazardous plan, but it would be far more dangerous to go looking for Luca without a weapon.

Ducking, I run across the meadow, past the flower beds, the mown lawn, and the tall loudspeakers, the wailing of the sirens piercing my eardrums. Then on toward the steps that lead to the front door. Rain lashes my face. I leap for cover behind a spruce. As I get my breath back, I look at the dark house, which stands there peacefully. Menacingly quiet.

I can't help thinking of Uncle Ole. The old postman stood on these same steps only a few days ago and said goodbye to Mother and Father with an uncertain smile on his lips. A few hours later, he was dead.

And it was my fault.

The light goes on in the sitting room. I flinch and dive back under cover. Peeping out warily from behind the tree, I see a familiar silhouette appear at the window.

Mother!

She puts her face to the glass and I retreat behind the tree, making myself as narrow as possible. Mother stares out into the garden. Her body starts to stagger. What's wrong with her? Mother looks drunk. But that's impossible; she doesn't drink. She hasn't for six years for fear of losing control. At least that's what she said to Father on her fiftieth birthday when he was going to pour her a glass of *grown-up fizz* to celebrate. I was nine at the time and didn't understand Father's surprised reaction. A slap.

I feel tense as I lean forward again and see a dark patch, about the size of a plate, on her apron. It's like the shape of Eastern Australia, the purple-colored country on our Risk board.

Is that blood?

Is Mother injured?

It's my chance at any rate. While Mother's in the sitting room I mustn't hesitate a moment longer. Pushing myself away from the tree with both hands, I race down the narrow sand path behind the house. Lightning strikes somewhere nearby. There's an ear-splitting crash and dazzling flash of light before it goes so dark again that I can barely see my hand in front of my face.

I crawl on all fours beneath the windows, right through elder bushes, nettles, and spiky branches before I finally get to the kitchen door.

I listen but hear nothing apart from the wind howling past our house. A loose wooden board clatters above me. I look all around, but there's nobody to be seen. Just darkness everywhere. And cold rain whipping my face. The orange-yellow light from the kitchen window picks out a glistening conifer. I nervily pull myself up and venture a glance inside.

I can't breathe.

Oh my God.

28

Blood everywhere! My horrified eyes jump from the trail of red in the hallway to the blood-smeared doorframe, the smudged fingerprints on the floor, a knocked-over chair, our wood oven. My mind can't process this gruesome picture.

What the hell has happened here?

Then I glimpse the shoes. I recognize them at once even though they're caked in mud. Luca! Those are his lace-ups. My stomach churning, I stand on tiptoes and take a better look. He's lying there, huddled by the sink in a pool of blood.

Tearing open the kitchen door, I storm in and throw myself on the floor beside him. My trembling hands stroke his face. Luca's eyelids flicker when he realizes it's me.

He's alive!

"Luca! For God's sake, can you hear me?" I whisper, hardly able to speak. He just looks at the kitchen door and groans in pain.

"She's in the sitting room," I say, staring again at his blood-soaked jumper. Luca's holding his stomach with both hands and wheezing.

"We need to get away from here right now," I whisper. The sight of him breaks my heart. "Can you walk?"

Luca just shakes his head weakly.

"Boy's on the boat," I say, my eyes full of tears. "He must've got to the other side of the lake by now and informed the guards." I gently stroke his cheek and sob from the depths of my soul. "They're going to come and save us, Luca. And call a doctor. Please, please hang in there!"

His eyes wander aimlessly across the room, then he looks at me again and nods, his face contorted in pain.

"We're going to get away from here. Promise," I whisper.

Luca shakes his head.

"Yes, we will," I answer. "You mustn't give up. I'm going to get you out of here."

He moves his head again, shaking it more vigorously. Rolls his eyes. Then he nods at me again and opens his mouth. He's trying to say something, but it's unintelligible.

"What?"

A gurgle comes from his throat. Luca grits his teeth, raises his chin, and then lowers it. Again and again.

I give an exasperated shrug.

"Thuh," he moans; it's barely audible. I lean forward and put my ear to his lips. A gently breath caresses my earlobe. "*Aaaa-rma.*"

"Arma?" I ask. "What does that mean?"

Luca swallows and screws up his eyes. The pain must be unbearable. He's gasping for air. His lungs make a strange whistling. Luca tries to speak; I lean in again.

My left ear brushes his lips.

"*Pistola.*"

Immediately I turn around and peer where he's straining to look. Now I understand what he's been trying to tell me.

It's lying on the ground, by the glazed crockery cupboard and next to the metal bucket with the cleaning cloths. Luca's pistol. It must have landed there during the struggle.

"*Pistolaaaa,*" Luca repeats, nodding feebly. Speaking is painful for him.

"I don't know how to use it," I whisper nervously.

"Take...it...*pron...prontamente.*"

A firearm. We children were strictly forbidden from touching Father's rifle. His holy relic against the strangers on the other side. We were only allowed knives. To kill the fish we caught, quickly and painlessly. That's the sixth commandment. But a firearm causes pain. And Luca's in severe pain; I can see how he's suffering. Father must have critically wounded him. Or was it Mother? My palms feel sweaty. Lost in thought, I wipe them on my wet jumper.

"Elly...*ti prego,*" I hear Luca plead faintly behind me.

"I...I can't."

"*Tua madre...non voglio...morire.*"

I don't understand the foreign words coming from his lips. But the urgency in his voice is perfectly clear. The danger lurking in the house. Overcoming my fear, I pull myself together, bend over and crawl toward our crockery cupboard. The pistol is within reach. Luca splutters; it sounds watery. I pause and turn to him. He gives me an encouraging but frail wink. Bright-red blood is dripping from his lips.

For a moment we gaze at each other, as if connected by a silken thread. The ticking of the cat clock above the fridge gets quieter, becoming more distant with every second. We don't need words to understand each other. My feelings for him. His feelings for—

All of a sudden, his eyes widen, and Luca gurgles blood. He tries to scream. Then I hear loud footsteps behind me, stomping like Schubert's Marche Militaire. In a panic, I turn around.

A black pair of ankle boots. So close to my face that I can count the dried spatters of blood on the leather.

29

Mother bends down and grabs the pistol. Then she stands back up and aims the barrel at my left eye. I jerk backward and hit my head against the table leg.

"Well, well," Mother says. "Our naughty girl is back."

"Please don't," I beg, holding my hands protectively in front of my face. Behind me Luca begins frantically rasping. His legs twitch on the floor. My body is shaking, too. The terror I feel paralyzes me, and I can barely breathe.

"What's that in your hand?" Mother steps toward me and points the gun at my closed fist.

I stare at my trembling fingers; I'd forgotten I was clutching something. All this time my left hand has been closed so tightly that the sharp object has become part of me. The skin of my knuckles is scratched and bloody.

Putting her head to one side Mother yells, "Drop it! Now!"

I open my fingers; Father's glasses fall to the floor.

"Where did you get them?" Mother asks, astonished.

"I found them," I stammer.

"Where?"

"Down by the shore."

"He's blind without them," Mother says, rushing forward to grab Father's glasses. Holding the frame up to her eyes, she examines the glasses as if they were some alien object. Then she slips them into the front pocket of her apron and looks at me thoughtfully.

"You found them, you say?"

I nod. Luca groans.

Mother aims the gun at my face again. "What happened, Juno?"

"I don't know, Mother."

"Don't lie to me," she spits, brandishing the pistol in the air. "Where is your father?"

I turn to Luca; he blinks. I don't have any choice but to tell Mother the truth. "Father...went into the water."

"Why?"

"Boy..." I stutter. "He...he went in a dinghy...over to the other side..."

"To the strangers?" Mother yells, aiming the gun at Luca. "How many of you are there on the other side?"

Luca gives a start. He tries to answer, but blood comes from his lips instead of words. Gurgling noises. Anxious, I rush over to Luca and hold him tightly in my arms. He feels cold. "Can't you see he needs a doctor?" I scream at Mother.

"What the stranger needs is medicine," Mother says, pointing the pistol at the granite mortar with the comfort pills.

"Go...Elly!" Luca gasps. "Run!"

"You're staying right here," Mother barks. "Unless you want to be responsible for his death."

"Stop, Mother!" I roar. "He's done nothing to you!"

Luca holds his stomach and doubles up.

"This stranger...wants to take my babies away," Mother snarls. "But you're a gift from God. The almighty placed you in my care as recompense for the fact that I can't have healthy children of my own."

"You abducted us!"

"We loved you. All these years. God helped us bring you up," she says, her voice cracking. "And only *He* may take you away again."

"You're ill, Mother!"

Luca begins rasping again.

"The comfort pills, Juno," Mother says, pointing undeterred to the mortar. "I'm not going to tell you again." Then she points the gun back at my forehead. "Free your new friend from his pain. Or would you like me to shoot him in front of your eyes? Like an injured racehorse?"

Sweat is running down my back, and I feel chilled to the bone. What am I going to do? My body is shaking. If I don't give him the comfort pill Mother will shoot us both.

"What are you waiting for?" Mother says, her anger brewing again. "Don't we want to see how well my medicine works? I didn't make it with so much love for nothing."

I hesitate and glance at Luca. His torso is full of blood. He's clutching his chest with both hands and groaning softly. I slowly get up and let my arms dangle, exhausted. Mother narrows her eyes, waiting for my reaction. But I don't move; I'm hopelessly looking for a way out. What am I going to do?

My fingers rub my jumper. And then I remember the comfort pills from the safe room, the *placebos*. I took two—they're going to save us.

I just have to get them out of the front pocket of my dress without Mother noticing. I pull the wet jumper over my head, and instantly freeze; the cold night air gusts in through the open kitchen door.

"What are you doing?" Mother says.

"I don't want to catch a cold," I reply nervously, dropping the jumper on the floor. "The wool is drenched. Surely you don't want me to get ill." The only argument I can think of that quickly. I pray that this can stir the last remnants of her maternal feelings. It seems to work.

Mother eyes me suspiciously. "OK, but hurry, now. We don't have much time before more strangers pitch up on our island."

"I'm...alone," Luca groans.

"Quiet!" Mother scowls.

I turn my back to Mother and stand at the work surface. In front of me is the granite mortar, filled to the brim. I make a show of reaching for the orange comfort pills with my right hand, while my left discreetly slips into my pocket and searches for the hidden pills. The cold, wet material wraps around my hand like ivy. My fingertips go deeper, desperately searching every corner of the pocket. But I can't find them anywhere.

"What are you waiting for?" Mother says, turning to me.

The sticky remnants of jelly and grainy powder burrow beneath my fingernails.

Oh no!

The pills must have dissolved in my pocket.

"Come on!" Mother hisses.

Hesitantly I take a comfort pill from the mortar.

"And now put it in your mouth, Juno," I hear Mother say close to my ear. "Surely you don't want to get ill. Show the stranger how effective they are."

Luca tries to get up. He seems to have a hunch that the balls of jelly are filled with poison tablets. I hear him panting, his legs kicking. His screams, doubled-up with pain.

"I can't," I sob. My entire body is burning. "Why? Why do you want to kill me?"

Mother laughs. "Come on; you're the one in our family who loves fairy tales. Can't you work it out for yourself?" She snorts. "Why did Hansel and Gretel's caring stepmother leave the children alone in the forest?"

"Because she was wicked!" I roar.

"No, my girl. She had her reasons like I do. Right, then. Put it in your lying mouth," she orders, jamming the barrel of the pistol into my side. "You're not my daughter anymore! No daughter steals from her mother. I've lost enough in my life! Do it!"

My fingers are shaking as I put the pill on my tongue. I close my mouth and my eyes, taste the fruity sourness of the coating that immediately spreads across my dry gums. In my head various images appear: our safe room, the bare bulb, the shelves, the preserves, Father's armchair, the rifle, specks of dust hovering in the cold dungeon.

"Swallow it!" I hear Mother order. I can still feel her pistol digging into my ribs.

I can't. I mustn't. I don't want to die.

"You've had years of practice, stop making such a fuss," Mother says. "Or do you want some help?"

I deftly maneuver the pill beneath my tongue and swallow demonstratively. Once, twice. Maybe that will trick her. I make one final, loud swallowing noise and open my eyes.

"Good," Mother says. "Is it down?"

I nod. She looks at me skeptically and sweeps a hair from my brow. A sweet and sour taste unfurls beneath my tongue.

"Open your mouth!"

I open it slightly.

"More!" she barks, pressing me against the work surface; the wood digs into my back. I wave my arms around in an attempt to grab hold of something. The pill wanders aimlessly inside my mouth.

"Go on, open your insolent little mouth!" she says, grabbing my jaw with her thumb and forefinger. "This is what they did with me! Back in the clinic!" Her sharp fingernails bore into my cheeks, forcing my mouth to open. "It works, believe me." The pain is unbearable, but I muster all my strength to keep my jaw closed and clench my teeth.

"Swallow!" she screams, incensed. "Swallow it down you filthy liar!"

The palms of my hands slap the work surface. I desperately try to get some purchase. Glasses tumble into the sink, soup bowls smash on the floor, my fingertips touch dishcloths, wooden spoons, soap. The pain in my cheeks gets worse. And then, finally, there's a solid object to hold. The granite bowl—the mortar with the pills.

"Traitor!" Mother howls; spit flies into my face.

Grabbing hold of the mortar, I swing it as hard as I can in front of me. The granite crunches into Mother's forehead, and the comfort pills go flying through the room like a broken amber necklace. One after another they patter on the floor.

Mother staggers backward, holding her head in astonishment. Her eyes are wide open, and blood is dripping into her face.

"You'll pay for that," Mother says, standing back up to her full height. "Is my own daughter turning against me?"

I hold my breath. How's that possible? The blow seems to have done nothing. She stands in front of me, weaving and wiping the blood from her eyes.

"And all because of him?" she asks, groaning as she raises her arm. I stare into the barrel of her pistol. Mother sways. I swallow, feeling powerless, paralyzed by fear.

"Because of a worthless stranger?"

"Luca isn't a stranger!"

"I see," she says. "No longer a stranger…to you?" She grins crazily. "I think you've fallen in love. How tragic." She now points the pistol at Luca. "So, my girl, let's see if you've been paying attention. How does our sixth commandment go?"

"Please, Mother! Don't" I beg her. "I'm sorry."

"Only sometimes it's not quick and painless," she whispers, pulling the trigger.

An agonizing cry. Luca rears up; blood spurts out of his thigh.

"Noooo!" I thrust out my arms and push Mother back. Taken by surprise, she trips over Luca's legs, wobbles backward, falls against the dining table, tries to push herself back up and puts a foot on the rug.

For a split second her eyes are as large as saucers and stare at me in horror. Then the rug envelops her like colorful wrapping paper and drags her down into the black hole.

A scream, a dull thud. A cracking sound like wood.

Then it's quiet.

Silent.

Exhausted, I creep over to the hole in the floorboards and peer into the darkness. She's lying there just a few meters below me. Motionless on the sandy ground, her body strangely contorted. I feel oddly sad.

I hurry back to Luca and wrap my arms around him. He moans, breathing heavily, pressing his hand on the wound in his thigh. I loosen my grip, unsure what to do. I gently lean my head on his shoulder. Suddenly I feel furious. Mother has no right to make me feel sorry for her.

And then I begin to cry. In sadness, in joy, in despair. My tears flow like water from an open tap. It feels good.

The emotional tempest raging inside me becomes calmer with every breath. The cramps in my stomach relax.

"Waa…di…you?" Luca grunts in pain.

"We've done it," I whisper, stroking his pallid face. "She's dead. Did you hear that, Luca? We're safe." I'm comforting both of us. Giving us hope, for a brief moment, at least. Even though I can't believe it myself. What if Father comes back? Luca's cheeks feel cold. "You've just got to hang in there. Please!" I beg him. "Keep going till Boy notifies the guards. Then they'll come over to the island!"

"Waa…what…di you…" Luca pants. Speaking is a real struggle for him. "What…did…you…?"

I lean forward, putting my ear to his mouth. "What are you trying to say, Luca? What did I…?"

"What…did…you do…with the…tab…let?" he groans.

I go numb. The comfort pill?

Feverishly I run my tongue around my mouth. Over my gums, inside my cheeks. It's gone! The tablet isn't in my mouth anymore!

I'm suddenly filled with dread. Did I spit it out somehow in the struggle? I search the entire kitchen floor for the pill, running my fingers over the floorboards, lie flat, swivel around and around, making me dizzy. Please God, I didn't…?

And then I find it! Behind a chair leg. The pill I've been looking for! Like a rotten yellow tooth. Relieved, I let myself slump against the kitchen door and stretch out my legs. I didn't swallow it. Thank God!

Beaming, I nod to Luca, pointing at the pill. His eyes follow my broken finger and he responds with a faint smile. I stand up and, as I go over to him, I feel a crunching beneath my shoes. Puzzled, I lift up my foot and look at the floor.

A scrunched tablet. How come there's another one?

In my mind I see the broken necklace again. Mother's comfort pills soaring through the kitchen. Everything is spinning. I hear a low droning, my eyes feel heavy, a swarm of hornets hovers just above my head, flashing blue lights mix with the howling singing of angels. Everything blurs, my fingers tingle, legs give way, the floor rushes toward me. I hit my head, no pain, I can't move. Just want to sleep, want to go, leave Northland forever. With Luca on the beach in Riccione, his hand in mine. Behind us a forest of towers rises into the turquoise-blue sky, where a shining silver bird does its rounds. Children's laughter. Pushing off with our feet, we begin to glide, heading toward the sun, the warm, golden-white light.

The kitchen door flies open.

A chorus of voices all around me.

Loud and confusing.

Foreign.

30

FIVE MONTHS LATER

Once upon a time there was a little girl who longed for her parents, because she'd been stolen by a wicked witch and taken off to a horrible island. One day she went down to the shore and said, "Oh, what I would give to be able to leave this hideous place forever." And she wept bitterly.

But because it was the old days, when wishes still came true sometimes, she saw something shining brightly between the trees. The girl thought it was the moon in the night sky, for it shone brightly, but in fact it was the face of a noble son of a king from a foreign country called Southland, who promised to save her.

She took fright from the black beetle that accompanied the prince, and wanted…

Putting down my pencil, I look at what I've written in my notebook. I need to use simpler words. Words I've already learned. *Mum, dad, family.* It still feels unfamiliar. I open my English book and look up the word for *Hexe*. After a while I find the translation and jot down *witch* in the margin. I'm dreading having to translate the entire text into English.

Once a week my parents take me to see Dr. Clarke, the aging child psychologist from the University of Cambridge. She suggested I write down my traumatic experiences in the form of a fairy tale. Like in *Thumbelina*, the story that's been with me all my life. They call it a *trigger*. It's how I'm supposed to learn how to process the fateful events. The *adjustment disorder* I've supposedly been diagnosed with. And with PTSD. At least that's what my English teacher said, who in the first few weeks helped out as an interim translator during my sessions.

I've been seeing Dr. Clarke alone for almost two months now. Every week I find it easier to make myself understood in her language. Express myself. It doesn't work with my true feelings. I'm still keeping them to myself, deep in my secret safe room. And it doesn't help if I have to write a silly fairy tale.

And she lived happily ever after.

Luca didn't live happily ever after. He died. And with him a little bit of me has died, too. The reality doesn't get any easier just because you write it down.

I shut my notebook. I'll have time to do it tomorrow. On the flowery cover is a bright-pink nameplate on which Mum wrote two words:

Elly Watson.

She cried when she did it. I pick up my pencil and scribble over the name until it's illegible. In disgust, I then scratch another name over it in big letters: *JUNO!!*

This is still Juno's story, not Elly's. I open the bottom drawer of my desk and put the notebook on the pile of newspaper articles that Dad collected for me in the first few months. In case I'd like to read them at some point when I'm ready. I haven't glanced at them once.

I hate this drawer.

Worn out, I kick it shut, lean back in my chair, and run a hand through my short hair. I was allowed to choose my haircut. From a picture book showing lots of different women wearing lipstick. All of them were laughing like crazy, as if it were the happiest day of their lives. Even though they'd had their hair cut off, too. I copied them and smiled at the girl in the mirror. But she looked like a stranger.

All the same, I'm recognized everywhere I go. They even showed my face on Dad's black box in the sitting room. Mum calls it *television*. It flickers away all day long. Usually Olivia's sitting in front of it, watching *cartoons*. A cat chasing a mouse. But the mouse is smarter and always gets away. I prefer the cat. He always loses, the poor guy.

Olivia doesn't care that the cat loses no matter how hard it tries. She claps her hands and squeals with joy at each mishap. Olivia's only four; she's my little sister. She looks more like me than Boy ever did. Probably because she was born in a hospital rather than being brought home from the supermarket.

I look at the picture frame decorated with hearts on the desk beside my butterfly orchid. I framed the pink piece of paper that the police gave me at the end of their investigation. For weeks they compared the folded piece of evidence they'd found in Mother's bloody apron with Luca's DNA. When I found out about this, I had to plead for ages to get the piece of paper. Mum was unsure, but good old Dr. Clarke argued in favor of it. Ruth's message would surely help the healing process. In the end my parents agreed. They cut off the dark-red stain in the corner with scissors.

I look at the two short sentences.

My big sister wrote them and hid the note beneath the cover of my fairy-tale book.

Fourteen words. And the reason why Boy hasn't been in touch with me for weeks.

One Sunday morning Mikkel rang me from Sweden, raving about the dwarf rabbit he'd been given as a present. And how happy he felt with his new family. How nice they all were to him. And how exciting it was when they visited some crazy zoo.

He talked so much.

But he didn't want to speak about our time on the island. Nor about Father's arrest when they pulled him from the lake, completely disoriented. Father's now in a German prison, awaiting trial.

I felt numbed throughout the entire phone call. As if that time had never existed for my brother, even though it will link us for the rest of our lives.

When, after what felt like an eternity, he finally asked about my life in England, I just told him about Ruth's message, the folded note in my book of fairy tales. He was surprised; he didn't know anything about a secret message. He tentatively asked me what she'd written. I sensed his uncertainty, suspected he didn't want to know the truth. About our island, Father and Mother, the other side, the strangers.

So I answered him with a question of my own: "What would you have written in two sentences if you'd had the chance?"

Boy didn't reply. I think he is angry that I didn't tell him what Ruth wrote. But it is her message to me, not him.

I hear a blackbird singing through the open window and can't help thinking of the conversation with Mother. When she talked about my big sister for the first and last time, before she threatened to let Boy drown in the lake. How could I know that Mother would reveal Ruth's secret message to me?

I think of Ruth's lucky black stone, lost somewhere on the island. Like a fragment of me. I get up, go to the long curtain, push it to the side, and look down at the street.

There's only the odd reporter outside, now. The police say it will be a few weeks before I can go out into the street in peace. To protect us from the English strangers, we hid in a hotel on the edge of the city when I arrived. Mum, Dad, Olivia, and me. Until an anonymous tip-from another guest made our secret public and there was no longer any point in staying there.

Again I'm a prisoner in my own house.

I watch a young woman with a microphone standing with a bearded man beside a little open bus. He's holding a heavy camera over his shoulder and filming her. Pointing at our house, the reporter makes a grim face. She's probably wondering how I was able to survive for thirteen years on the island with Mother and Father. The answer's rather banal. I just did. I just functioned, as my therapist Dr. Clarke likes to say, similar to the war children in Afghanistan. But what does she know? Afghanistan isn't Northland.

Other people are standing around the reporters, most of them my age, but also frail types like Uncle Ole, some with little dogs on leads. They're taking photographs of our front door, too. With their *cellulares*.

I can't help thinking of Luca. Of our first night by the shore.

When the stranger came. And became a friend.

I give a sudden start. There it is again—the sound! Above my head. The swarm of angry hornets is going wild. The low buzzing on the island, just a few meters above me, in our kitchen. It's getting closer and closer. I close my eyes and see flashing blue lights. I count slowly from one to ten. Gently exhale through my nose, focus on my breathing, just like Dr. Clarke taught me.

It's only a helicopter, I think, trying to reassure myself, only a helicopter. You were rescued by one of those, Juno. At the last minute, just in time, before Mother's comfort pill... Breathe, it's a good sound.

There's a knock at the door. I open my eyes.

"Yes?" I say, turning around in a daze. The door to my bedroom opens a crack, and I can smell the powdery aroma of vanilla and rose petals.

"Can I come in, Elly?" Mum says softly, entering my room. There's an anxious smile on her lips. She comes a few paces closer and opens out her arms. "I heard the helicopter and came straight up—"

"Thanks Mum," I say, going over to this stranger. She puts her soft arms around me and strokes my back lovingly. I begin to sniffle.

"I'm really so sorry," she whispers, pressing me closer to her warm body so I can feel her heart. "I imagine that this whole adjustment has been very difficult for you."

I give a faint nod and taste salty tears. We stand like this for a few minutes until she breaks free from our embrace. The sweet fragrance of her rose-petal perfume wafts up my nose. She tenderly wipes my damp cheeks. "We're a family, Elly. You can always tell us the truth. We can talk about everything, like with Dr. Clarke." The woman begins to weep. "I love you so much, Elly. Do you think you'll ever be able to feel at home with us here?"

"Yes," I answer quietly. "I think I will...Mother."

My right forefinger stays silent.

READING GROUP GUIDE

1. In the opening chapters, Juno loves Mother's comfort pills. What was your first impression of them? What did you learn about the medicine by the end of the story?

2. Initially, Juno's world seems almost dystopian. What did you make of it, before the truth was revealed?

3. Ruth, Juno's big sister, managed to swim across the lake before she died. What do you think she did on the other side? Why do you think she came back?

4. Why do you think Juno so quickly becomes attached to Luca? What do you make of her feelings for him? Do you think they are reciprocated?

5. Discuss the role of fairy tales in the story. What purpose do they serve for Juno and Boy? Are they helpful or harmful?

6. How does Juno's own story compare to the traditional fairy tales of the Brothers Grimm, such as *Hansel and Gretel* or *Little Red Riding Hood*?

7. What are Luca's motives for helping Juno?

8. Consider how easily Boy reacclimates to life after the island. What makes Juno's transition into her new family so difficult? Do you think Juno can be happy in this new life? Why does Juno say "Mother" instead of "Mom" to her birth mother at the end?

9. In your opinion, does the book's ending qualify as "happy"? If not, what would you have wanted for Juno?

10. Did you figure out what was written on the pink slip? (Hint: The solution is in italics on page 166).

ACKNOWLEDGMENTS

First of all, I would like to thank you from the bottom of my heart for reading my novel. That means a great deal to me. Even as I am writing this note to you, it still feels like a fairy tale that my debut novel, which was published in Germany in the summer of 2022, has found its place at such a wonderful U.S. publisher and that you can now hold it in your hands. German novels rarely make it across the Atlantic, and I still can't believe how lucky I have been.

On this incredible and unlikely journey across the ocean, the novel and I have been supported by countless wonderful and talented people. Their number is too big to thank all of them by name, yet I would at least like to express my gratitude to some of them, representative for all their colleagues. From the bottom of my heart, I would like to thank Dominique Raccah and my editor, Jenna Jankowski, at Sourcebooks, as they believed in my novel from the start and worked closely together to bring out the best in this text.

I thank the wonderful Jamie Bulloch from London, who translated my debut novel, working closely with me. My gratitude goes to my German friend Thomas Scholz, PhD, who learned all about comparative literature at Washington University in St. Louis and took on the role of adaptation editor, supporting me with his knowledge of creative writing, translations, and great stories.

Thanks to Spencer Fuller of Faceout Studio for the great cover. I love the design and illustration!

Thank you to my wonderful literary agent, Marc Koralnik, of Liepman AG in Zurich and the Blake Friedmann Agency in London. Without you, my debut novel would never be available worldwide. You made it possible!

Writing a book is a very lonely job. You sit in your dark cubbyhole and see nothing of the world for months. That's why I thank my wife, Nadine; my daughter, Ava; and my mum, Hanni, for their spiritual support during the writing process. I love you guys!

Thanks also to my wonderful test readers, Kerstin Neidhart, Joachim Ziebe, Christopher Heinzerling, Bernd Nieschalk, and Tom Rust from Portland, Oregon. Like running a marathon, you guys cheered me on every chapter. That's what kept me going.

And last but not least, I would like to thank the people who have always inspired me during my creative phase: Gillian Flynn, M. Night Shyamalan, Steven Spielberg, David Fincher, Shonda Rhimes, Jason Starr, Michael Crichton, J. J. Abrams, Margaret Atwood, Stephen King, John Williams, and Shirley Jackson. You are my role models; thank you for your wonderful works!

If you enjoyed my novel, I would love for you to email me at hello@ivarleonmenger.com or follow me on Instagram: @ivarleonmenger.

Ivar Leon Menger

Summer '23

ABOUT THE AUTHOR

Ivar Leon Menger, born in 1973, is an award-winning German author. He holds a degree in graphic design, was a copywriter at the U.S. advertising agency Ted Bates, and has worked as a director for films and fiction podcasts. His Audible original series Monster 1983 (Golden Record) and Ghostbox are among the most successful series in Germany. He works in Berlin and lives with his family in Darmstadt. More at ivarleonmenger.com.